# CONJUROR

JOHN BARROWMAN is an actor,
a recording artist, a presenter and
Carole's wee brother. He's best known
for playing Malcolm Merlyn/Dark
Archer in *Arrow* and Captain Jack
in the television series *Doctor Who*
and *Torchwood*.

CAROLE BARROWMAN is an English
professor and the Director of Creative
Studies in Writing at Alverno College
in Milwaukee, Wisconsin, and
she's John's big sister. Carole and
John have collaborated on
six books together.

Also by
**JOHN AND CAROLE BARROWMAN**

*Hollow Earth Trilogy*

The Hollow Earth

The Bone Quill

The Book of Beasts

*Orion Chronicles*

Conjuror

# JOHN & CAROLE
# BARROWMAN

# CONJUROR

HEAD
ZEUS

First published in the UK in 2016 by Head of Zeus Ltd

9 7 5 3 1 2 4 6 8

A catalogue record for this book is available from the British Library.

ISBN (HB): 9781781856376
ISBN (XTPB): 9781781856383
ISBN (E): 9781781856369

Typeset by e-type, Aintree, Liverpool

Printed and bound in Germany by
GGP Media GmbH, Pössneck

Head of Zeus Ltd
45–47 Clerkenwell Green
London EC1R 0HT
WWW.HEADOFZEUS.COM

*To teachers everywhere*
*and*
*with love to Adeline Beatrice Murray*

# PROLOGUE

The first Conjuror came to America in a slave ship. In 1797 a lone ship drifted up a tributary of the Mississippi. Alonzo Blue, overseer of the Dupree Plantation, spotted the two-decker bobbing in the choppy water. As word spread of the ship's strange arrival, the field slaves vanished into their damp huts, closed their shutters and shoved pellets of hardtack into their ears. They knew what was coming.

At dusk the voice of an angel singing a wordless aria could be heard, like the fluting sound of the breeze through the sugar cane, or the delicate notes of the harpsichord in the big house's front parlour. The music floated from the ship in a pulsing silver mist, above the moss-draped oaks, through the rubber trees dripping with wet lichen, dipping and darting across the indigo fields until it reached the party at the plantation house, where handsome guests were sipping sweetened rum from tulip-shaped glasses on the wide veranda.

At the cool touch of the mist, the guests' fingers twitched, their limbs stiffened, their eyes fluttered and their glasses fell to the wooden planks of the porch. The women's ears trickled blood on to the lace of their white cotton dresses. The men's collars sliced into the throbbing veins in their necks.

The music stopped.

# FIRST MOVEMENT

# 1.

# EL DIABLO WEEPS

SOUTHERN SPAIN, 1510

Tears of joy creased the powdered cheeks of the Grand Inquisitor Cardinal Rafael Oscuro as he listened to the boy sing. Tugging a perfumed kerchief from the sleeve of his gown, he dabbed at his eyes, and then crooked his finger at the man in red and gold silk lounging on a chaise behind the child.

Don Grigori finished his sugared square of marzipan and glided across the chambers towards his master, his gait surprisingly graceful for such a tall man. Blond hair curled at the curve of his elegant neck, framing the youthful face that audiences across Europe courted and coveted.

He kneeled before the older man.

'Your Eminence?'

Don Grigori's voice was as high and girlish as his cheeks were smooth. It was a voice that could make the heavens smile – if Don Grigori had been interested in such mundanities.

At the twilight of his second decade, the Vatican's most famous *castrato* could still hold a note for minutes and the attentions of princes and popes for hours. He had been a gift to Rodrigo Borgia from Spain's emissary at the Vatican when, as Pope Alexander VI, Borgia had granted the kingdoms of Castile and Aragon to Spain. Don Grigori's fame had grown even as popes had fallen.

The Grand Inquisitor gestured for Don Grigori to rise.

'Where did the boy come from?'

The child's ankles, visible beneath the hem of a sackcloth tunic, were clotted with welts from months in manacles. His fists were clenched at his sides. The boy was biting his lip. The boy was trembling. But the boy was not crying.

Don Grigori stood again, licking flakes of sugar from his rouged lips.

'He arrived two days past from the Ivory Coast, Your Eminence.' He had adapted the pitch of his high voice with a lilting cadence that was mesmerizing whether he was speaking in Spanish, Italian, French or English.

'Was he alone?' asked the Grand Inquisitor.

'He is now, Your Eminence.'

'His age?'

'It is difficult to say. His diet has been poor.'

'A guess then?'

'Not yet in manhood.'

The Grand Inquisitor smiled his approval. 'Excellent. We are in time.'

The child was, in fact, ten years old and, until he had been hunted like a wild boar and forced naked into the rat-infested hold of a slave ship, had been well-nourished and deeply loved.

The Grand Inquisitor cupped his hand under the boy's chin. The boy jerked his head away. 'Ah, we have a spirited one. Does he have the mark?'

'I could not find it, Your Eminence.' The *castrato* paused, before adding, 'I examined him... thoroughly.'

'Still, with a voice like his we cannot take chances.' The Grand Inquisitor ran his manicured fingers over the boy's roughly shaved head. 'How did you find him?'

'The Moor was protecting him. I had a spy placed in his household days ago when he first became a nuisance. Her presence finally bore fruit.'

'Ah, Don Grigori, my most loyal friend, you will be doubly rewarded.'

Don Grigori kissed the Grand Inquisitor's lips. It was a dutiful kiss, one to seal a promise rather than sustain a dalliance. Those desires had ceased for Don Grigori years ago with the nip of a knife.

# 2.

# A FALSE EDEN

The Grand Inquisitor stepped on to his balcony and inhaled the perfumes of his gardens. A warm breeze rippled the sparkling water in a chain of ponds, where faceless human statues cavorted with odd reptilian creatures. A great phallic fountain with a blue globe at its base soared at the centre of this secret garden, designed for the Grand Inquisitor's eyes alone. Every tree in the garden was heavy with strange, lush fruits, and creatures that had no place in the world outside frolicked in the foliage. Perched on a drooping branch, a peculiar, oblong-shaped owl stared back at the Grand Inquisitor with wide, lidless eyes.

The Grand Inquisitor regretted what he had to do, but he had spent too long in this place enjoying the hospitality of the Spanish Inquisition. The Moor, Don Alessandro de Mendoza, was drawing close and he couldn't afford to have his plans exposed. He must retreat once again, let his network of soldiers and spies continue under Don Grigori's leadership, while he rested and rejuvenated. After all, time was the Grand Inquisitor's closest ally. As for the Camarilla, they were as ancient as the Knights Templar and their mission just as sacred. With Don Grigori at the helm, the Camarilla would be ruthless and unwavering.

With one last lingering look at the view, the Grand Inquisitor reached under the stiff collar of his robes and lifted an ivory pitch pipe to his lips. He played a note and held it for a long beat before releasing it.

The sound raked over his glorious garden. Tines of yellow light turned over the soil as if under an imaginary plough, and cyclones of dirt swirled into the air, each leaving dark holes in the ground. From each cavity a swarm of scarlet flying beetles, the size of dragonflies, burst from the earth to hover in a thrumming cloud above the Grand Inquisitor's false Eden.

He put the pipe to his lips again. Now the red swarm mowed over the landscape like locusts, devouring everything, reducing the garden to a wasteland of sticks and stones, shattered statues and contorted limbs. The Grand Inquisitor surveyed the scene with a frown.

Behind him, Don Grigori cleared his throat.

The Grand Inquisitor tucked the pitch pipe on its velvet ribbon under his collar.

'It is good we leave here, Don Grigori,' he said. 'We have grown too comfortable in this time and place.'

'What do you intend to do, Your Eminence?' A stray

beetle fluttered in from the garden, landing on Don Grigori's exaggerated cuff. He flicked it off with a long finger. 'The Moor's sorcery is strong. My spies tell me even our Queen trusts him intimately. And I fear he has others of his kind within his immediate circle.'

'The Moor's persistence has exhausted me. I should have listened to you, my friend. We should have left this place sooner.' The Grand Inquisitor squeezed Don Grigori's shoulder, the gesture close to an apology. 'However, I have arranged to correct this indulgence. Our portrait is almost complete. I think I'd like to venture west. Perhaps explore the new world beyond the horizon. We appear to have worn out our welcome in this old one. A ship bound for Hispaniola waits at Marbella for us. The ship's captain belongs to our trusted Camarilla, and has been well compensated. He and his crew will ensure our slumber is protected during the journey.'

'What of the Moor, Your Eminence?'

The Grand Inquisitor smiled coldly. 'Others are dealing with him and his cabal as we speak. He should not trouble us for much longer.'

'And the boy?'

The Grand Inquisitor considered his options. Such a truly divine voice, but without the mark the boy was merely a distraction. He poured two goblets of wine and held one out to Don Grigori.

'If the child does not bear the mark, then he is worth-less to me, but the Vatican choir will be the richer for his voice.' He brushed the back of his hand across Don Grigori's soft cheek. 'Especially since the Pope has never forgiven me for stealing you away.'

'I'll take the boy below,' said Don Grigori, pausing to savour the rich red liquid in his goblet.

The boy whimpered. It was the only sound he'd made since he'd stopped singing.

'And remind the barber he is no longer the village butcher,' added the Grand Inquisitor. 'If he is not more precise in his cuts, he will be retired. Permanently. The fool has made far too many mistakes of late. It was likely one of his slips of the blade that brought the Moor's attention to us in the first place.'

'I will take care of this boy personally,' said Don Grigori, draining the goblet. 'It will be my pleasure. And perhaps one day he and I may sing for the gods together.'

The child's whimpering cries suddenly rose up in a series of notes that shocked the older men. The goblet fell from the Grand Inquisitor's hand and smashed on the shining tiles as a visible whip of sound threw Don Grigori against the nearest wall like a ragdoll.

'Why, you—'

The Grand Inquisitor raised his hand to strike the boy, but the song was too beautiful, too seductive, too pure, too divine. His imagination tilted. Tendrils of fog snaked at his feet, paralyzing him in his velvet slippers. His overfed body swayed to the aching melody while his mind struggled against the music as it swelled in a silver mist around him.

'Silence… him!' The Grand Inquisitor gasped. 'He has the mark, he must… Don Grigori, silence him!'

But the *castrato* lay slumped in the corner, his long legs splayed uselessly in front of him, leaving the Grand Inquisitor fighting to purge the boy's voice from his imagination alone. The effort was sapping his concentration. He could not make his hands do what his brain wanted of them. Helplessly, he raised his fat fingers in the air as if conducting the ribbons of sound swirling around his legs.

Don Grigori groaned as wraithlike vapours of perfect music carpeted the chamber, reaching across his fallen body and pressing him to the floor, the melody slowly squeezing the air from his lungs.

Blood wept from the Grand Inquisitor's eyes and ears. 'Who has trained you?' he gasped, fighting on. 'Whom do you serve?'

The boy's voice only rose higher, shattering the gilt-framed mirrors on the walls and the crystal decanters on the table, raining shards of glass. A dense curl of mist wrapped around the handles of the balcony doors and flipped the key from the lock.

The Grand Inquisitor's vision was a blur. Tearing his pitch pipe from under his robes he dragged himself to the balcony windows, pressing his free palm to the glass and blowing feebly.

At once the scarlet beetles rose from the charred earth and charged the balcony doors like a million tiny red arrows, coating the panes in crushed shells and dark inky blood.

The boy sang on.

The Grand Inquisitor jiggled the gold handles hopelessly, his sweaty hands slipping, his fleshy elbow thumping into the stained glass over and over again. This century's appetites had weakened him. Full of bile and riddled with gout, he had become soft and lazy, his powerful magic muted. In desperation, he blew once more into his pipe. This time the beetles rose off the balcony and formed a battering ram, their scarlet shells gleaming in the midday sun, to pummel the door over and over again until a web of cracks spidered across the thick glass.

The frenzied fog of sound whipped around the Grand Inquisitor's neck, his chin, his face, enveloping him, pressing the pipe against his pocked chin. He toppled to the ground, his body mummified in a web of ropey fibres, leaving only one eye left to stare at the boy through tears of blood.

The balcony doors shattered.

# 3.

# PERFECT PITCH

The beetles encased the boy in seconds, filling his mouth, clogging his throat and choking his voice. He swallowed some and spat out the rest in sticky clumps. Shaking as many off as he could manage, he twisted his robe up over his head, knotting it off like a hood. He mustered a rondo, a repeating phrase he'd learned years ago from his father before he died in a hunting accident, the melody rushing from his imagination.

But the beetles and his exhaustion were winning. The mist and its effects were beginning to dissipate. And Don Grigori was stirring. The boy collapsed to his knees, his voice faltering. Groaning, the *castrato* reached for his mummified master.

With an explosive splintering of wood the chamber doors burst open and a tall, brown-skinned soldier crashed into the room, wielding a sword in each hand. His breeches were tucked inside black riding boots, knives sheathed on their silver buckles, and his head was wrapped in a low yellow turban. Opals pierced his ears and a fist-sized golden tablet etched with peculiar glyphs rested at the glistening V of his open tunic.

Two of the Grand Inquisitor's household guards leaped into the chamber after him. The soldier pivoted, lunged at the guard to his left, piercing his neck. Before the first guard fell, the soldier feigned a counter-parry, cross-stepped, and lunged at the second guard, stabbing through the hatch in his armour and piercing his heart. The second guard dropped instantly. Smelling fresh blood, a horde of beetles abandoned the boy's head and flocked to the guards instead.

The soldier sheathed his swords. He quickly took measure of the mummified Grand Inquisitor and the stunned *castrato* before striding to the boy he'd rescued from the slave blocks at Cadiz two months since.

'Damn you, Moor,' croaked Don Grigori.

'I was delayed, child,' said the soldier, soothing the boy with his mind as he spoke in a mash-up of Spanish and Swahili. 'I regret it most bitterly.'

Pulling down his makeshift hood, the boy threw himself into the Moor's arms and pressed his face against the leather bands that criss-crossed the soldier's loose white tunic.

Don Grigori suddenly lunged for the Grand Inquisitor's pipe on the floor.

The Moor put the boy aside, pulled a blade from his boot and, with a brutal swiftness, chopped off the long fingers on the *castrato*'s right hand. Don Grigori flew backwards, howling, his blood spraying the velvet-papered walls.

Fat with the flesh of the slaughtered guards and Don Grigori's severed hand, the beetles swarmed once more around the boy's head and mouth, insatiable in their bloodlust. The Moor pivoted back to the child, calming his small, trembling body and settling his terror as the beetles flew about them both in thick bloody clouds.

Through a gap in the swarm, the Moor's dark eyes caught Don Grigori struggling to lift the enchanted ivory pipe to his own thin lips.

'Boy!' The Moor hissed. 'Sing again, before it is too late!'

But Don Grigori blew on the pipe at exactly the same moment as the boy opened his mouth and struck a perfect high C. Their conjuring rose up in two great dissonant waves of sound, colliding in a blinding white explosion of music and marble.

# 4.

# SMOKE IN THE AIR

O n the red mountain bordering the Grand Inquisitor's garden, the artist gasped, yanked off his skullcap, dropped to his knees and prayed. He then sat back on his haunches and took a sip of ale, then another, and one more for good measure from the pouch fastened at his waist. What had he witnessed? When the sounds had collided, it was as if the earth shifted inside the Grand Inquisitor's chambers with a force so powerful the rear of the palace had collapsed.

He secured his pack round his waist, and climbed quickly from the rocky ledge before jumping the last few metres on to the narrow path that led to the outer wall of the palace, or what was left of it. Ducking behind the remains of a woodshed, the artist waited, but no guards appeared. No one from the village would risk life or limb to come to El Diablo's rescue. The palace and its walled grounds were eerily silent, the air heavy and dry, as if the explosion had created a vacuum to which sound had yet to return. As far as the artist could tell, he was alone.

He ran to the slabs of broken marble and mounds of rubble beneath what was left of the balcony. Staring up at the destruction, he weighed his chances. It would take him, a man deep in his fifth decade, far too long to climb unassisted. What if he should fall or – worse yet – get trapped in the twisted wreckage?

The artist sighed. He did not take lightly what he needed to do. He had to finish this commission, whether the Moor had survived or not. And that meant he would have to animate.

He unfolded a torn piece of parchment, stretched the cloth out on the cracked stones, licked his wooden pencil and drew with great haste, his imagination working to its limits. Steps appeared one after the other, rising in a fat line of blue light from the mosaic-tiled path up into the collapsed chambers.

The artist took them two at a time into the Grand Inquisitor's lair.

# 5.

# WHAT TO DO

Inside the chamber, the air was thick with dust and grime that coated the artist's mouth and throat. He couldn't see the boy amid the chaos. He couldn't see the Grand Inquisitor or Don Grigori either. He prayed they had both been squashed as flat as the dead, scarlet beetles that carpeted the room.

Clambering over the rubble, he saw a hand sticking out from beneath what was left of an iron and wood chest. The chest had snapped in three places, the heaviest part pinning the Moor beneath its weight.

The artist used his own sweat and muscle to lift the broken wood and iron from the Moor's chest. It wasn't enough. The Moor's legs were pinned by something bigger, something the artist couldn't move.

He kneeled by the Moor's turbaned head, which was caked in blood from a gouge slicing through his eyebrow into his scalp. Pulling a paint rag from his pouch, the artist did his best to clean the blood from his friend's face. He pressed his hand to the Moor's chest, but his fingers were shaking too much for him to feel a heartbeat over his own racing pulse. Instead he leaned his ear to the man's lips and listened.

Nothing. Wait. Something. A ragged whistle of air? Perhaps.

Quickly, the artist used a chunk of brick and sketched a pouch filled with water on the ground. It burst from the thick air in an oval of blue light, and landed with a splosh next to the Moor. It was all he could do, other than pray – and complete the mission on his dear friend's behalf.

He searched quickly until he found the box, the size of a small saddle with the design on the wax seal identical to the mark he had concealed with black ink at the curve of the slave boy's neck. Securing it under his arm, the artist scrambled back to the balcony and down to the foot of his imagined stairs, where he dug the scrap of parchment from his pouch and rubbed out the drawing. The steps dissolved to nothing in a whizzing zigzag of blue light.

# 6.

# NOT EVEN A CROAK

The boy waited until the artist was gone before he climbed wearily back up to the broken chamber, his whole body aching from where the explosion had blown him clean over the balcony. The Moor was still breathing, but only just.

For the first time since his capture, the boy wept. Then, as he brushed his arm fiercely across his eyes, he noticed a water pouch with a strange bluish hue sitting off to the side. He lifted the pouch and poured water over his own shaved head first, catching the drips with his tongue, before pouring some on the Moor's forehead. The Moor's eyes fluttered. With hope leaping in his thin chest, the boy poured more water directly into the Moor's mouth.

The Moor, Don Alessandro de Mendoza, gagged as the water rushed down his throat. The boy dropped into his arms, mumbling incoherently with relief. Gently, groggily, the Moor calmed the boy with his mind. After a moment he touched the boy's throat, then pointed to the mass pinning his legs.

'Can you get me out, child?'

The boy placed his palms flat on the mass of marble resting on the Moor's legs. He inhaled and released. Not a sound came out, not even a croak. His terror was blocking his ability to conjure the music. He needed help. More power.

Shifting himself into a less painful position, the Moor lifted the golden tablet from around his neck, set it on the ground beside him and, with the hilt of his knife, cracked it in two. He placed the half still on the strap around the child's neck, tightening the leather a fingertip from the child's blood mark. He kissed the boy's forehead and nodded, tucking the other half of the tablet into the loose folds of his own shirt.

'Again. Try again.'

The boy touched the tablet and tried again.

This time he inhaled more deeply, the way his father had taught him. He let his heart and his head fill with light before releasing a string of crisp, clean notes. Like the swift current of a river, the music coiled around the marble, lifting the debris inches off the ground. It was enough for the Moor to tug his legs free.

The deep gash in the Moor's calf was still bleeding. The boy watched in a daze as the Moor tore a strip of cloth from his yellow turban and tied it tightly around the wound. He picked up his sword from the rubble and sheathed it, scooped the boy wordlessly into his arms and leaped over the broken balcony to the ground below.

The boy was so drained by the music that he was struggling to stay awake. He felt himself being placed gently on the saddle of a great horse tethered at the palace gate, then felt the great bulk of the soldier vaulting on to the saddle behind him. They galloped down the path together into the hush of the red mountains.

'Such sweet compulsion doth in music lie.'

*John Milton*

# SECOND MOVEMENT

# 7.

# SOME KIND OF FREAKY

The sign swaying above the shop's door read, 'Old Worm's Curiosities and Ancient Alchemies'. Tucked in a narrow cobbled alley not far from the Strand, the latticed windows were filthy, concealing the curiosities inside. Rémy Dupree Rush pushed open the heavy wooden door. He winced as the bell jangled, the noise cutting into the low-level thrumming in his head that had led him here. He adjusted his guitar case, settling it against the middle of his back. He cranked the volume on his iPod and flipped up his hood. Static rather than tunes fizzed in his ears, electronic configurations of white noise. The low frequency held the thrumming to a more tolerable background noise.

A stocky white dude in a cardigan and corduroys and a middle-aged woman with red-pencilled lips looked up from their desks, assessing him. Skin surveillance, he called it. Happened all the time in Chicago. Why would London be any different? It didn't matter that he was wearing his dad's expensive Belstaff jacket, that his shirt was clean and pressed and his boots spit-polished, Rémy Dupree Rush was a young black man shopping.

Ignoring their lingering stares, he scanned the interior. Given how far from normal most of his seventeen years had been, he was prepared for weird, but this was some kind of freaky.

The shop was long, narrow and poorly lit, with low oak beams. A standing fan kept the stale air moving, fluttering the edges of some 1851 Great Exhibition bunting advertising 'The Wonder Room of the Wicked'. A curved balcony papered with ancient yellowed maps hung above the congested ground floor. Animal skins, a stuffed vulture, horns of polished ivory, owls with milky glass eyes, a ferret with two heads and a preserved polecat caught Rémy's eye. Drawers with labels in Latin were everywhere he looked, dust motes swirling where light breached the shop's shadowy interior.

The keening in his head from the tablet around his neck grew louder. He bit the insides of his cheeks to stop from crying out. Clearly he'd found the right shop.

He walked past tables packed with specimen jars and almost knocked over a pine coffin filled with a dozen tiny mummified bodies in ruffled collars and cuffs. Skirting barrels and buckets with calligraphic labels marked, 'Lizards' and 'Mice', 'Snakes' and 'Miscellaneous', Rémy noted shelves that buckled from the weight of oversized manuscripts, thick, leather-bound books and more stuffed creatures. The shop smelled of pipe tobacco, damp wood, and old.

For a second Rémy was transported to Tia Rosa's balcony looking out over the muddy Bayou Teche, where she'd sit smoking Tupelos, drinking Kentucky bourbon from a china cup and listening to jazz. Tia Rosa had milk crates stacked with vinyl classics of jazz, blues, Zydeco and Louisiana Creole. When they had all fled Louisiana, Tia Rosa had sold most of her albums. She deposited the money into a peanut butter jar behind her headboard for Rémy's university fund. He'd taken the cash when he'd left.

Rémy yanked out his ear buds. The static wasn't helping any more. The thrumming was so loud that it was hurting his teeth. As he headed towards a door marked 'No Admittance', the beat in his head trebled and the thrumming golden tablet around his neck burned his skin. He lifted the tablet out and over his shirt. Nestled into a corner of the shop, he spotted a tall antique cabinet with a brass lock.

He loosened the strap on his guitar case. The tablet was now a full-on orchestra of pain. From the corner of his eye, he saw the shop assistant with red-pencilled lips nod discreetly to the man with the cardigan, who walked quickly to the door and locked it.

Rémy felt a sting of satisfaction. Truth be told, Rémy Dupree Rush was thirty days, two deaths and one dark conjuring beyond giving a fuck.

# 8.

# PLAY SOMETHIN' SWEET

CHICAGO

FOUR YEARS EARLIER

'Let's make somethin' sweet for your birthday breakfast, RD.'

'Sure, Mom,' said Rémy. 'What'd you like to hear?'

'How 'bout my favourite?'

Annie Dupree Rush leaned against the chipped Formica table and closed her eyes. Her nappy hair lay plastered against her scalp from the heat, the skin under her eyes dry, her lips cracked, her skinny body wrapped loosely in a pink chenille robe. Rémy watched the deep lines of sadness on her brown skin smooth away as her lips settled into a soft curve, her head tilted back and her slender fingers tapped out a beat on the counter.

'You are my sunshine, my only sunshine,' she began. 'You make me happy when skies are grey...'

She flicked her other hand towards Rémy as if conducting an orchestra, not her only son sitting at a wobbly, Formica table with a guitar on his fourteenth birthday. A stream of light flashed from her fingers. Rémy blinked, not sure what he'd seen.

And then everything changed.

For most of his life, Rémy had heard music in his head: fragments of orchestrations, bursts of notes, riffs of chords and melodies. Sometimes the sounds blurred his vision and, on occasion, disrupted his senses. Rémy would see and feel impossible things, velvet between his fingers when there was no velvet to be had, taste peppermint when a violin played. When the music distorted his connection to reality in this way, he'd shut down. Tia Rosa and his mother would let him be, but at school he was the weird kid, the kid with 'special needs', the labels and his own withdrawal alienating him from the rest of the world.

As he got older, Tia Rosa's lessons on controlling his responses to the music in his head – teaching him how to look less catatonic – began to pay dividends. One day in fourth grade, Rémy realized he could use the structures of sound, the patterns and the images of the music he imagined, to solve a math equation with an elegance that shocked his teacher. From that day on the labels 'gifted' and 'high on the spectrum' were added to his permanent record, alienating Rémy even further.

But even at its most extreme, the music had never altered reality the way it did that morning.

His mother's singing slipped from rough gravel and sand to smooth whipped cream and sweet-potato pie. The music became lines of colour and light in Rémy's mind, with his mother's voice like a thread looping and linking them together, until the images moved outside his head and floated above the table like holograms of old family movies.

There was Rémy aged eight singing a solo with the Chicago All-School Symphony; playing spirituals on his grandfather's guitar in a New Orleans' church at five; as a toddler in his high chair blowing tunes on a penny whistle. Then the pictures stuttered as though the film had snapped, scattering the ghostly images across the kitchen. They weren't Rémy's memories any more. They were his mother's.

His mother as a teenager taking a bow in a great red and gold music hall, a bouquet of roses in her arms, the audience on its feet, her eyes bright with excitement and then, in a flash, brimming with tears of shock and fear when she suddenly recognized the shape of the tattoo on the wrist of a man in the front row, the roses scattering at her feet. A cloud of silver mist burst from Annie, reaching towards Rémy.

'You'll always know, dear, how much I love you…'

The whole kitchen – the cracked white ceramic sink, the stove with its single working burner, the wheezing, green fridge – wavered in front of Rémy's eyes, and filled with dancing waves of silver. The bands of sound shimmered with each note, warm and sticky on Rémy's skin. He felt his mother's voice opening his mind, teasing his imagination, freeing the powerful voice that lived there, the strange sorcery he knew now had always been within him. Then Rémy too began to sing.

'No! No! Stop!'

Tia Rosa burst into the room, her eyes haunted and horrified. She skidded to her knees, tugging at the ragged hem of her niece's robe.

'Don't do this to the boy, Annie! He won't be able to come back from this. They'll find you! They'll take him...'

But it was too late. For admonishments. For anger. For regrets. The genie was out. Pandora's box opened. The apple bitten and shared.

# 9.

# STICKY FINGERS

The song and the sound dissolved like morning fog on Lake Michigan, leaving a stack of hot pancakes drenched in blueberry syrup in the middle of the table. Rémy stared. Had he just conjured food from music?

'Aw, that's lovely, RD,' Annie said, sticking her finger in the purple syrup and dribbling it into her mouth.

Tia Rosa wiped her tears on her sleeves and faced her niece. Even her ropey grey cornrows were shaking with fury. Sweat glistened on her copper skin. She slapped Annie hard across the jaw, knocking her head back, snapping her teeth into her tongue. Blood joined the blueberry syrup coating Annie's lips.

Rémy jumped from his seat, reaching for his great-aunt's hand. 'Tia Rosa, don't hit her—'

'Sit down, son.' Tia Rosa's voice was as hard as granite.

Annie spat blood into the sink.

'It was time, Rosa. Boy's been ready for a while and you know it. He deserves to know 'bout his kind and get prepared for what's to come.' She ran the faucet, cupped water to her mouth and drank. 'And I'm tired… so tired of all of this.' Her hands swept over the room. 'Sick of the voices in my head and his evil always clutching my heart.'

'Mom, who are you talking about?'

'Not you, Rémy,' Annie said. 'Never you. You were the best thing I ever created. And you're stronger than me. Even now. You're stronger than me, baby boy. You always have been. When your voice changes and you're a man, you'll be able to conjure without anyone's help. And you'll succeed where others in our family failed. I know it. I truly know it.'

She laid her head on his lap, and began to sob. 'I can't do this alone any more, baby boy. I just can't.'

# 10.

## OUT OF WORDS

'Don't cry,' Rémy said helplessly. 'Mom, please… it's OK…'

His mother pulled herself up, rubbed her face with her hands and fled from the kitchen. Rémy and Tia Rosa flinched at the sound of her bedroom door slamming shut, the key turning behind her as it always did.

'What the…? What just happened, Tia Rosa?'

His aunt picked up the pancakes and syrup and slid the mess into the rubbish container under the sink, plates and all. When they hit the bottom, they disappeared in a flash with a sound like a hammer on a xylophone. Then she dug behind the garbage disposal and uncovered a bottle of bourbon, pouring two fingers' worth into two mugs.

'Drink this. It'll calm your nerves.'

Outside the window, a plane from O'Hare banked over the horizon. Rémy wished he was on it, going anywhere far away from this kitchen. He coughed as the bourbon burned his throat and seared out across his chest. On the only occasions he'd drunk before, it was on the balcony late at night with Sotto, and it was a can of Budweiser. This was liquid fire.

He asked the question he was most afraid of.

'My mom isn't human, is she?'

Tia Rosa reached across the table and took his hand, squeezing his fingers in hers. Her hands were rough from a lifetime of teaching violin and cello to children before taking on his and his mother's care full-time.

'She's human, son,' she said. 'But she's something else as well. And so are you.'

'The music…' Rémy stopped. How was he supposed to put any of this into words?

'Like your mom, your imagination is hard-wired in such a way that you can create things, alter reality, when you play or sing, Rémy,' said his aunt.

If Rémy hadn't witnessed the transformation in the kitchen less than an hour ago, he would have decided Tia Rosa had climbed on to the crazy train with his mother. But in his heart, he'd always known his differences ran deep. He'd read music before he'd read words, plunking out melodies on a plastic piano at three. By the time he was seven or eight, Rémy could play any musical instrument he laid his hands on. He'd listen to a song on the radio, hum a few bars and then riff on it, expand it and make it his own. He'd taught himself the harmonica listening to Big Walter, Howlin' Wolf, John Mayall,

Stevie Wonder and Bob Dylan, the blues guitar from Muddy Waters and BB King. Music was as much a part of him as his blood and bones.

'So Mom and I can create things with music?' he said aloud. 'Like, say, pancakes and blueberry syrup?'

When his aunt nodded, Rémy furrowed his brow.

'So I'm a freak,' he said.

His aunt pulled a Tiparillo from a pack in the drawer and rolled it between her fingers. She'd given up smoking years ago, but Rémy had noticed that the feel of the tobacco on her fingers, the last vestiges of her habit, calmed her.

'You're not a freak, son. You're a Conjuror,' she said. 'To my knowledge, you and your mom are the only ones left in existence. Your father was one too, God rest his soul. Perhaps their marriage was unwise,' she added, almost to herself. 'That combination of power... I worried what it would lead to.'

Rémy gripped the edge of the table. He wasn't in any mood to think about his dad. He never was.

Tia Rosa gave a brief shake of her head.

'There are others who can conjure, son. But unlike you and your mom, they can't use their voices, just certain sacred instruments. They've had lots of names since the beginning of time – Afriti, Moloch, Scaramallion, Lucifer. It's said only a powerful Conjuror can destroy them. Needless to say, they don't much like your kind.'

Rémy felt a cold prick of fear. For years now, pretty much since the death of his father, his mother had been growing more distant, more obsessive, more paranoid. She had kept him away from kindergarten, walked him to and from school, stayed by his side more than most mothers. She saw monsters in shadows, threats in conversations, violence in a handshake. Now the monsters and threats and violence, it seemed, had a name. Evil.

He gulped the last drop of bourbon.

'Then let's hope I never run into one of these demons,' he said. His head felt light. 'Because I'm not ready for battle.'

'Even with the controller that's glued to your thumbs?'

The terror in Rémy's head dissolved a little. 'Maybe killing it on Mortal Combat is a transferable life skill after all,' he said with half a smile.

Reaching up, he touched his finger to the raised birthmark on the back of his neck. It was a little larger than a thumbprint. God's stamp of approval, his mother always said. The devil's mark, his grandfather would counter. After this morning, Rémy was leaning towards his grandfather's view.

'The Conjuror's mark,' said Tia Rosa. 'You know your mom has it too. It's special.'

'Grandpa didn't think it was so special.' Rémy lowered his hand. 'Mom's curls in a different direction from mine.'

Tia Rosa's eyebrows lifted. 'Well now, I never knew that. I guess I'm not as observant as I thought. Still, a Conjuror's mark is a Conjuror's mark, no matter what way it spins. Your grandpa's only education on conjuring was the stories he heard from his mamma, who heard them from hers, and so on and forever back to the time when the first Conjuror arrived in Bayou Teche on that demon slave ship.'

Rémy fingered his birthmark again. It bothered him suddenly that it wasn't exactly the same as his mother's. He couldn't remember his father's mark, whether it had curled to the left or to the right. His stomach gave a familiar clench. His memory of his dad was an abstraction, a longing, a series of detailed imaginings where he pondered what his life might have been if his dad had survived the hit and run.

His aunt was watching him. 'Do you remember when your father died, Rémy?'

'No,' said Rémy lying.

'You were five.'

Rémy fought the memory, but it came regardless. He had spent the day with his mother at the Dupree Plantation archives, reading *Curious George* at a table big enough to live on. His mother had surrounded herself with ledgers and journals, poring over iron-brown handwriting, notes of sale, accounts and wills and all the paraphernalia of the museum. He remembered being alone in the great dark rooms of the plantation house, long windows striped with moonlight. He remembered fear in his belly. How had he got there? And then there had been a crash outside and a scream and he had been alone.

'Are you sure you—'

'I'm sure, Tia Rosa,' he said, more sharply than he had intended.

The bourbon was taking its effect on his elderly aunt. Her eyelids were fluttering and she was fighting to stay awake. She stared groggily into her almost empty mug.

'When your mom was born and your granddaddy spotted the Conjuror's mark on her shoulder, he banished her to Bayou Teche to be raised by his sister,' she said. 'When Bessie got too old, I went to help.'

This was safer ground. Rémy felt the tension ease from his shoulders.

'I remember Tia Bessie,' he said. 'She'd give me rhubarb stalks dipped in sugar.'

'Bessie did her best by your mom, that's for sure. She educated her well, and allowed her to play her music without shame. She taught her to embrace her gift. Unlike your granddaddy.'

'What do you mean?'

'That old man didn't interpret the mark in the way Bessie and I did. To him, it was a sign of Satan, a symbol of evil simmering in your blood. He banned music from the house and wouldn't let your mom play or even listen, for fear she'd incite the apocalypse and bring on the reign of Beelzebub.'

'What if he was right?' said Rémy, his pulse quickening. 'What if being born with the Conjuror's mark is a bad thing?'

'No child is born bad,' said Rosa. 'But there is a darkness here, son, that I still don't understand. It's a shame you don't remember the day your father passed on. A shame...'

'A shame in what way?' Rémy asked cautiously.

The answer was so faint he almost failed to catch it.

'Because I think your momma saw something in the archives of the Dupree Plantation that changed everything for her. And I think you saw it too.'

Outside, Chicago's traffic honked and steamed and stank. Rémy turned over his memories, trying to find anything that would match what Tia Rosa was describing. All he could bring up was an image of two men standing in a room. No – one had been sitting down.

Tia Rosa seemed to wake up. 'I found you that day, you know,' she said suddenly. 'Asleep, curled up under a four-poster bed in a plantation bedroom. You must have wandered away from the library.'

Rémy's head almost burst with the effort of remembering. He saw the men again, one standing and one sitting. Their faces wouldn't slide into focus.

'When your mom was climbing into the ambulance with your dad that day, she was hysterical,' said Tia Rosa. 'She kept screaming that I protect you and "destroy it". I figured I'd do the protecting part and worry about the destroying some other time.'

'Destroy what?'

Tia Rosa shrugged her shoulders.

'Whatever it was that she saw, we left Louisiana that day and never went back. I'm sure your mom has details somewhere but...'

She fell silent. They both knew what she was thinking. That Rémy's mother hadn't let anyone see her research in almost ten years. Hadn't even let anyone into her bedroom in about as long.

Tia Rosa stroked Rémy's cheek. 'Despite everything that's happened, baby boy, you and your mamma are the gold in my life.'

Rémy watched his aunt drag herself slowly towards her bedroom. He closed his eyes. Behind his lids he saw the memory of a hand-held battery fan, blue and plastic, spinning like a whirligig at the feet of a man with a hessian sack at his shoulder, a pitch pipe in his mouth and black flies buzzing above his head. As he squeezed his eyes tighter he heard an oboe and a snare drum, like a heartbeat and a howl.

# 11.

# COUNT TO TEN

*One Mississippi. Two Mississippi.*
Rémy rolled his neck muscles, double-checking his surroundings.

*Three Mississippi. Four Mississippi.*

A man in a navy pea coat, his collar turned up against the chill, stepped into Old Worm's Curiosities and Ancient Alchemies. Nodding at the shop clerks, he jogged up the wooden staircase to the balcony two steps at a time. Rémy took his mother's notebook from his inside pocket and flipped to a page he'd marked with an elastic band. He glanced at the series of scrawled drawings and ragged photographs she had torn from an auction catalogue just a few months ago.

*Five Mississippi. Six Mississippi.*

The cabinet matched the drawings and photographs. Relief flooded Rémy. He was in the right place.

*Seven Mississippi. Eight Mississippi.*

For the first time in his seventeen years, Rémy Dupree Rush was OK with validating a racist stereotype. He pulled his hoodie over his buzzed hair, making sure it covered the mark on his neck, then stared as menacingly as he could at an elderly lady browsing a stack of musty books in a nearby aisle. Clutching her handbag to her chest, she scampered away, muttering under her breath.

*Nine Mississippi. Ten Mississippi.*

In a blur of movement, Rémy dropped to the floor and popped open his guitar case. He grabbed something inside and stood up.

'He's got a gun,' someone screamed.

Fear. The most powerful weapon of all.

# 12.

# NO DIRTY NOTES

Rémy Dupree Rush did not have a gun. Instead he gripped a harmonica, a blues harp, a Reckless Tram, a Mississippi saxophone. While the shop clerks stood frozen with indecision, he began to play.

The music slid from his head to his hands. No slurring notes. No dirty chords. His was a clean melody. Rémy's breathing deepened, his pulse slowed, but his nose began to bleed. He'd never animated so many times within short periods since he fled Chicago. Colour rose like streamers from his harmonica, curling round the rafters before dipping down and bouncing along the planked floor.

At the sound of the music, the clerks and customers turned like automatons towards the door. As Rémy picked up his tempo, so did they. No panic, no toppling over the macabre displays, no trampling over the buckets or barrels, no crazed frenzy. All was quiet and orderly as they filed out on to the street.

When everyone was safely outside, Rémy slumped to the floor, slipping his harmonica back inside the guitar case and snapping it closed. His head was pounding worse than anything he'd ever experienced before, and the tablet around his neck was still hot against his skin. He exhaled slowly, and then wiped his hands across his bleeding nose. Slowly, his imagination began to settle, the music in his head fading to the edge of silence.

As he stood up, the floor tilted, a million floaters filling his field of vision. Making his way unsteadily to the front door, he turned the lock. He rubbed at the dusty window with his sleeve and peered outside. The customers had gone, leaving just the two clerks huddled together on the kerb, talking into the woman's phone.

He leaned against a barrel of white bones until his legs steadied, then headed back to the antique cabinet. Shakily pulling on a pair of black gloves from his jacket pocket, it took him two tries to manipulate the brass catch and open the doors.

Inside on the left was a fretwork of drawers. Rémy ignored them, running his gloved finger along the top of the frayed satin lining at the back instead. A vibration shot up his arm, and a horrible *squeeee* exploded inside his head like air rushing from a balloon.

He pulled away. *Jee-zus*.

The din continued. After a moment, he tore away the corner of the lining, touching, pressing, squeezing.

Nothing.

He touched his finger to the tablet at his neck. Its regular thrumming and heat had brought him to this shop. It couldn't be wrong. He tore again at the lining. Nothing.

The man in a navy pea coat charged at him from nowhere with a Taser.

No time to think, only to act.

Rémy dodged sideways, pivoted and straight-kicked, knocking the man on to his back and sending the Taser skittering across the floor. Scrambling to his feet, the man rushed at him again. This time Rémy dropped his shoulder, let his guitar case slide down, grabbed its neck and swung it like a baseball bat into the side of the man's head. The man went down hard.

*Sorry, dude.*

As Rémy dragged him against the wall, he noticed the tattoo on the inside of the man's wrist.

*Shit.*

He knew that shape – three fat curved lines with a slash above and below, like a silhouette of a harp.

# 13.

# RUN, RÉMY, RUN!

The man was unconscious, blood oozing from a gash above his eye where he'd face-planted on to the floor. Of course the Camarilla were tracking him. He'd been dumb to think otherwise. They'd probably been on his tail since he'd fled Chicago. Maybe before.

Rémy slid to the floor. He was so tired. The tablet around his neck was still screaming, taunting him. He missed Tia Rosa and his mom. A sob escaped from his throat. He lashed out in frustration, kicking the pea-coat guy's legs multiple times until the man groaned and slipped back into unconsciousness.

Squeezing back his tears and letting his pulse settle, Rémy felt his anguish thin out. He pulled himself up, shored up his grief, stifled his self-pity and pushed on.

Outside, sirens were closing in on the shop, lights from the panda cars pulsing through the latticed front windows. A customer must have called the police. He had to move. Rémy pulled the unconscious man across the shop and pushed open a hobbit-sized door tucked into the rear wall. He dragged the man inside the cramped space, and then backed out, shutting the door and jamming a chair under the handle. He kicked the Taser under a cabinet, out of sight. He didn't need to be caught on the streets with it.

*This may not be Chicago, but he wasn't born yesterday.*

The male shop clerk was outside peering in, a uniformed police officer in silhouette behind him. Rémy sprinted up the stairs, out through a small arched window and on to an old iron fire escape. At last, the tablet stopped shrieking in his head.

He shut the window behind him. Rémy secured his guitar case on his back and climbed up the iron steps to the uneven roofs above the alley.

A loud whistle carried above the city's noise. A young police officer stood in the street below, staring up at him and talking into her radio.

'This is Patrol Officer one-zero-three in pursuit of a black youth, approximately eighteen years old, heading across the rooftops towards the Prêt-A-Manger on Adelaide Street. Repeat, a possible burglary suspect fleeing on the gabled roofs above Hogarth Lane...'

Rémy ducked behind a rusty water tank and crawled to the end of the roof, where he watched as the officer sprinted to the front of the old building. He could hear her yelling at the shop clerks. From the sound of things, they were being deliberately unhelpful.

'How do I get up on that roof?'

'Why'd you want to do that?'

'Is there a key to get into this place?' she asked.

'We're waiting for the owner to open up. He's always bloody late on Mondays, 'specially if he had a rough weekend.'

Rémy peered over the edge of the roof. The police officer was eyeing the clerks.

'Do you often turn up for work without coats or bags?'

'I don't see that it's any of your business.'

'Fine,' said the officer. 'You two stooges stay where you are. I'll be back for a chat in a bit, and you'd better have figured out a way inside by then.'

Rémy jumped across the roof to the building next door. But he wasn't fast enough. The officer was directly beneath him, looking up. In a panic, he scanned up ahead, trying to find the best way down.

A second officer was approaching the first, coffee in his hand.

'What the hell took you so long? Didn't you hear me whistle?'

'Sorry, Lakshmi, not a peep. What's up?'

'Spotted a guy climbing out on to the roof up there. Could be one of the jewel thieves mentioned at watch this morning.'

Exploiting the distraction, Rémy turned back the way he'd just come, and then scrambled to the building directly next door. The sound of a soprano practising scales in the building below wafted up through a filthy skylight. The woman's voice gave him pause, the music calming him a little. He looked down to an empty alley no bigger than a hallway, and across to the church of St Martin in the Fields.

The roof was newer here and the slates steadier. He backed up four steps and sprinted towards the building's edge. He leaped, his legs bicycling in mid-air, his guitar case banging against his back. He landed on the flat, tarred roof of one of the church outbuildings. There was no cover. Quickly, he shimmied down the shortest wall to the pavement below and ducked into an empty doorway at the rear of the church.

Car horns, a plane overhead, a cacophony of city noise, but no running footsteps and loud police whistles. Rémy glanced out from his hiding spot. Although it was still early on Monday morning, rivers of tourists streamed along London's labyrinth of narrow alleys. He burst from his hiding place, sprinting along the lane towards Orange Street.

*Wrong move.*

'Stop!'

Rémy skidded round the corner into the lower end of St Martin's Place, not slowing until he'd reached a throng of people. Yanking off his hood, he dodged deep into a pack of white teenagers. Another wrong move. He had no cover among the fair-skinned tourists.

'Stop that kid in the hoodie! The black kid with the music case! There!'

Rémy bounced off the tourists like a bumper car, ignoring the shouts closing in behind him. More police appeared. Ducking low, he snaked through more pedestrians, quickly cutting towards Leicester Square.

Rémy dropped his shoulder and rammed into the female officer on his tail. Instead of going down, she whipped out her baton and cracked it on the back of his legs. He leaped at the pain, but it jarred him on. With a second burst of wind, he charged into Irving Street and scrambled into an empty newsagent's doorway. He reached for his iPod. It wasn't in his pocket.

*Damn it!*

He must have dropped it.

*Criminal mastermind. Not.*

Still they came for him. Rémy picked up his speed, skidding on his knees behind a row of litter bins. He could see only one way out.

*You're stronger than I ever was, baby boy.*

Rémy filled his head with sound, imagining in a speeded-up film in his mind what he needed to do. Then he stood up. Rolling forward on the balls of his feet, Rémy lifted his head and began to sing.

'*Nessun dorma! Nessun dorma! Tu pure, o*
    *Principessa,*
*nella tua fredda stanza,*
*guardi le stelle*
*che tremano d'amore, e di speranza!*'

The swarm of police stopped. Pedestrians and tourists gawked as if a pause button had been hit. Rémy's rich tenor voice was pitch perfect and completely unexpected.

> 'Ma il mio mistero chiuso in me;
> il nome mio nessun sapra!
> No, no! Sulla tua bocca lo dire quando la luce
>    splende!'

A swirl of silver mist began coiling around Rémy's feet and legs, drifting up over his jacket and around his guitar case. He punched into a sprint, heading towards the statue of Shakespeare at the centre of Leicester Square. Adrenalin exploded into his limbs as he was enveloped in a shimmering silver shroud.

> 'Ed il mio bacio sciogliera il silenzio
>    che ti fa mia!'

The crowds faded, the police blurred. Rémy ran faster, sang higher, stretching himself out to the music, opening up the sounds in his throat, letting them carry him towards the statue.

> 'Dilegua, o notte! Tramontate, stelle!
> Tramontate, stelle! Al'alba vincero!'

Translucent pencil beams of light pierced the leather of his boots. All around him an ethereal sheen appeared to pillow the square. His hands became a shimmering bronze glow. His fingers fused together. A wall of sound morphed into a matrix of light. Each line pulsing, changing colours, striving for its crescendo.

*Here goes everything, Mom!*

In three bounding steps, Rémy got big air.

*'Vincero! Vinc-e-e-e-e-e-e-ro!'*

At the ear-splitting, bone-chillingly beautiful high C, every person in the square was brought to their knees, hands pressed to their ears, their cries competing with the final lingering note.

Their pain played to Rémy's advantage. Only a handful of people actually witnessed him defy the laws of physics and disappear into the now mist-covered statue of Shakespeare.

# 14.

## WHAT DYING SOUNDS LIKE

Rémy fell fast. His limbs felt loose, boneless, his guitar case pressing into his back as his music carried him through the solidity of the earth. Sensing the end of his fall, he lowered his pitch, slowing his descent, and skidded to a stop in shallow sewer water in an abandoned World War Two air-raid shelter, far below ground level.

With considerable effort, he dragged himself up against a damp wall. The music flattened to a throb in the back of his head, but his breathing was coming in shallow bursts. If he didn't get control of himself, he'd hyperventilate and pass out.

Needing a distraction, he picked up his harmonica, but he was too scared to play again so quickly after what had just happened. Instead, he held the harmonica away from his lips and went through the motions. Fingering the spaces, flexing his lips, filling his cheeks with his breath. He repeated the movements until he felt calmer, his imagination still.

His left ear was bleeding. He pulled his shirt cuff from under his jacket and wiped it. Even such a small movement caused his stomach to somersault as if he'd just stepped off a roller coaster. Leaning over, he retched, his body heaving violently into the curve of a sewer pipe. Then he tucked his knees to his chest. His head was filling with a cacophony of screams, as if the past inhabitants of the shelter were packed in with him, bereft for the lost world above. Flashes of light flared like white-hot sparklers behind his eyes. Rémy rocked in anguish.

*This is what dying sounds like.*

When the noise finally stopped and the pain dropped to a dull ache behind his ears, he put a shaking hand to the tablet at his chest. It was cool to the touch. He inhaled and exhaled slowly and deeply until his racing pulse settled and he could think clearly again. The Professor was right. Sometimes a deep breath was like an angel's caress.

Thank God for the Professor.

If it hadn't been for the Professor's help, Rémy didn't think he would have survived beyond his first days in London.

Before making his way into the city from Heathrow, he had busked for an hour outside the Tube entrance to earn some cash, using an old McDonald's cup to collect the money. He didn't want to risk using the pre-paid Visa card he'd bought with Tia Rosa's cash any more than he had to. He was more worried about running out of funds than running into the Camarilla. He didn't think he'd been followed across the Atlantic. Given the man in the peacoat, he now knew he'd misjudged.

A young goth couple, with tats crawling up their necks and down their arms, stopped to listen. They were thin but they looked clean, no twitching limbs or hollow expressions like the junkies that often gathered in the stairwell of Rémy's apartment building back home.

'You're pretty good,' said the girl.

'Thanks,' said Rémy.

He began another song. Later, when he was packing up he spotted the couple again, leaning against the opposite wall, watching him.

The girl approached, held out her hand. 'Cassie. This here's my cousin, Seymour.'

Rémy shook her hand and smiled cautiously at Seymour. 'RD.'

'Do you have a place to stay tonight, RD?' Cassie said.

'Sure I do,' Rémy said warily.

'If you change your mind,' said Cassie, handing him an address written on the back of a receipt. 'It's not the Savoy, but we'd find a space for you.'

'I don't have any money.'

'Rent's negotiable.' Cassie grinned. 'You could, you know, sing for your supper.'

Remy knew something was off with these two, but his eyes were burning from a lack of sleep and his whole body ached with grief and loneliness. Despite his misgivings, he said, 'OK. Thanks.'

The flat was in a condemned building in Croydon. Inside, the floor was carpeted with old mattresses and one or two foam yoga mats. Teenagers in various states of unconsciousness lay on top of most of them, some tangled in couples, others curled up like children, their arms flopped over their eyes. The few windows were draped with black bin bags. The filthy flocked wallpaper was damp and peeling, hanging from the walls like loose skin.

In the corner next to the bathroom, someone had rigged up a hot plate beside an electric kettle and a jar of instant coffee. Crouched nearby a kid, not much older than eleven or twelve, was licking the inside of a can of beans.

Someone had written, 'ALWAYS KNOCK TWICE' in black marker on the bathroom door. The place reeked of pain and hopelessness. Rémy didn't need any more of either. He couldn't stay.

Rémy waited until Cassie and Seymour were snoring on the tartan sleeping bags next to him. Then he crept down the stairs. Before he squeezed out through the loose boards barricading the door, Rémy took out his harmonica. He closed his eyes for a second before playing a soft bluesy melody.

He hoped everyone liked lasagne.

# 15.

# BLACKBIRD

The second and third nights, as he tried to figure out what to do, Rémy slept in parks and busked during the day at the entrances to Tube stations. On the evening of day four, he overheard a commanding voice lecturing from on top of a milk crate in the cobbled apron in front of Paddington Station.

The Professor was a tall, black man wearing a scholar's flowing robe, as if he'd stepped out of a lecture hall. Beneath that, he had layered a T-shirt, two cardigans and a brown hooded raincoat with a Union Jack scarf tied like a cravat at his neck. He wore sunglasses, fingerless gloves and stiff dress pants that could have walked on their own. But it was his voice that enthralled Rémy and the crowd that gathered to listen to him.

When he finally took a break, he strode over to Rémy and regarded him.

'Young man,' he said, 'do you know "Blackbird"?'

'Never heard of it,' said Rémy, picking up his guitar case. 'But I'm a quick learner. Why are you asking?'

'It's one of my favourite songs. I'd be willing to share my shelter with you in return for your musical accompaniment before and perhaps after my lectures.'

'You want me to be your warm-up act?' said Rémy.

'If it suits your busy schedule.'

The Professor hummed the tune. Rémy picked it up swiftly. The melody waltzed on the breeze, and people turned to listen.

'Ah,' sighed the Professor as Rémy played the final notes. 'They don't write them like they used to. Now, come with me. I have food.'

Since conjuring the lasagne at the Croydon squat, Rémy had found he was unable to create anything edible. Perhaps it was fear, or exhaustion, or a dread of calling attention to himself. Whatever the problem, it meant that the rumble in his stomach had been growing louder. It seemed as if the Professor had heard it. His attention and concern was making Rémy feel better than he had felt in ages. The screaming in his head since he fled home softened.

'Sure you're not a weirdo?' he checked first, slinging his guitar over his shoulder.

'I am the sanest man in London.'

For some reason, Rémy believed him. 'Deal,' he said, offering a fist-bump.

'Young people today are most extraordinary,' said the

Professor, regarding Rémy's fist, his robe flowing around him like a hero's cape.

Rémy discovered quickly the Professor was an important man to know if you wanted to survive off the grid. The man knew the underbelly of London better than any archaeologist. He was able to travel from Covent Garden to the catacombs beneath St Paul's faster than any taxi or bus. He travelled the length and breadth of the city at night with the cunning and grace of a sewer rat, sometimes taking Rémy along and sometimes not. After three days sharing his tunnels and his tent, Rémy decided that he was either a genius or truly nuts.

The Professor gave talks outside Paddington Station twice a day, rain or shine, audience or nought, about everything from the best place to get fresh veggies in the winter to the Peasants' Revolt in England in the Middle Ages. With his soft baritone voice and his sharp insights, Rémy figured in another life the man had been a history teacher.

His storytelling reminded Rémy of the Baptist minister from Texas his mother used to watch on late-night cable when she couldn't sleep. She would drop to her knees in front of the TV, praying for release from the demons that lived in her head, begging for salvation through the transmission of pixels and sound and the preacher's bright white smile. Rémy would tent his blankets, shove cotton balls into his ears and compose melodies and jazz riffs in his head. He had believed then the salvation his mother was seeking wasn't coming from God or Jesus, the Holy Spirit, or any other religion. He believed the deliverance his mother sought was from her own mind.

Man, was he wrong.

# 16.

## TACO TUESDAY

For the last three years in Chicago, Rémy had made it his mission to be normal, to fit in, to conform. Most of all, he had worked on not calling attention to himself or his mother. You never knew who was watching. Birthdays came and went unnoticed by everyone but Tia Rosa, who put a hundred dollars a year into his university fund, regular as clockwork.

Over those years, he shot up in size and muscle tone, diminishing the bullying and the taunting to the point where he could almost have considered himself popular. Almost. Of course, it didn't hurt that his landlord Sotto Square was a bad-ass. The local thugs tended to lay off when Sotto had a word.

His life had become copacetic until his seventeenth birthday. That day Rémy stayed after school in the band room with a couple of band mates, finger-picking a complicated jazz arrangement on his guitar. With no warning, he blacked out. As the world shut down, he slid from his seat to the floor.

'Dude! You a'right?'

Rémy looked up groggily. 'Thanks, man. I'm good.' Floaters were packing his peripheral vision like bombers in a video game. 'Lunchroom tacos not sitting well.'

'I hear ya!' His bandmate flipped his backpack over his shoulder. 'I can give you a ride home if you wanna leave now.'

'Naw, man. I'll be fine. I'll walk. Fresh air will help.'

'Fresh air?' His friend snorted, heading to the door. 'Where you goin'? Montana?'

Rémy packed up his guitar and his sheets of music. His stomach churned noisily. *Aw, shit.* He dashed to the bathroom in time to lose his lunch.

At the sink, he splashed water on his face and cupped handfuls to his mouth. Then he studied himself in the mirror. He had his dad's hazel eyes and sharp features, dimples softening his expression, but his mother's complexion: a blend of African, Spanish and French.

He ralphed a second time into the sink.

This time, as he cleaned up, he heard singing in his head. The melody was clear, but the song's tempo was slow, mournful, a mezzo-soprano voice coloured with melancholy.

'*You are my sunshine, my only sunshine...*'

'Mom?' Rémy said aloud.

'*...when skies are grey*'

Something was wrong with him.

With her.

Rémy ran from the building and chased the city bus
as it pulled away from the stop. He scrambled into the
first empty seat, his feet and fingers tapping to his mother's voice in his head, his heart racing and his palms
sweating. He checked his phone. No messages. No texts.
Nothing. Dread began melting his insides.

'*You'll always know, dear, how much I love you…*'

He sprinted across the street towards his apartment
block, dodging heavy traffic on North Avenue. At the
kerb, he checked his phone messages again. Nothing from
Tia Rosa, which was unusual. She didn't like to leave his
mother alone in the apartment for long. If she needed
anything before Rémy got home, she'd text him with a
list of grocery or pharmacy needs, some legal, some not
so much. Pot tended to help keep his mom's crazy at bay.

Avoiding the lift, Rémy sprinted up the stairwell. His
mother's voice was louder in his head now, trembling
with agitation.

A bluebottle fly the size of a bat buzzed passed his
head.

*Jee-zus.* He ducked and kept climbing.

At the third-floor landing, the temperature dipped,
crystals appearing when Rémy exhaled. The mark on
his neck tingled. The air here was heavy, something bad
lingering in the stairwell, a darkness echoing in the ether
like the reverb of a chord from his guitar.

The fourth-floor landing was colder still, the hallway long and L-shaped, his apartment the first one after the turn. Another bluebottle flew at Rémy's head. He swatted it and the giant fly smacked into the wall behind him with an almost human scream.

*Holeee shit. What is happening here?*

Another fly blasted into the side of his head. Two more slammed against the peeling paint on the walls and screamed afresh. Rémy bobbed and weaved through them, nausea in his throat, skidding to a stop outside the apartment door.

The sight and the smell crashed his senses.

# 17.

# LORD OF THE FLIES

The entire door was encrusted in bluebottles, thousands of them, each one as big as a fat fist. He couldn't see the latch, let alone fit his key inside. The air smelled like petrol and puke and tar.

Rémy pounded on the apartment door. 'Mom! Tia Rosa! Let me in!'

'Run, Rémy! *Run!*' His mother screamed as a million red, compound eyes turned on him. Rémy pulled down his guitar case and wielded it like a baseball bat as the flies attacked. Frantically, he pulled his hoodie up over his head, covering his nose and mouth. But the flies were beneath the fabric, crawling into his ears and up his nose. He pulled his harmonica from his pocket, slid it beneath his hoodie and played.

The flies fell from his face and his body at the first notes, the rest swarming above his head like a thundercloud, unable to penetrate the shield that the music had created around him. Forcing his way into the apartment, Rémy slammed the door, leaving as many of the flies outside as he could.

The apartment had been destroyed in a struggle. More flies coated the ceiling, dripping like tar down the walls. The stench of sulphur and iron was overwhelming. Keeping the harmonica to his lips, Rémy scrambled over the upturned furniture, shoulder-charged his mother's door and stumbled into a room he hadn't seen in twelve years.

The bedroom looked like the lair of a serial killer. Photos, clippings, notes and drawings covered the wall opposite his mother's bed. The other walls were papered in sheet music, ballads and blues riffs, lines of concertos and pages of unfinished symphonies. Every surface held towers of papers and files, books and documents. The bluebottles here were hovering like buzzards in clouds of blackness, waiting to feed.

Annie was standing on the rickety wooden balcony of her bedroom, leaning against the rusty railings, facing a sliver of Lake Michigan just visible in the distance. The hem of her sheer nightgown was blowing around her knees. The railing was not going to hold her weight for much longer. Her sobs punctuated the soft melody she was still singing.

'*I dreamt I held you in my arms…*'

Rémy ran to her. He was on the balcony before he realized his mistake.

'It's a pleasure to see you again, Rémy.'

The French Creole pronunciation of his name, in a voice that sounded like Louis Armstrong sucking helium, sliced into him like a razor. A tall ethereal figure glided between Rémy and his escape, flicking the harmonica from his hands and out over the balcony. Rémy's mother redoubled her song, leaning farther over the railing, as if on the prow of a sinking ship.

'Who the hell are you?' Rémy said.

The figure's feet weren't actually touching the wooden balcony, but hovering centimetres above it on a thick pillow of flies.

'I thought perhaps you would remember me,' he said. 'We met when you were a child at the plantation archives.'

Rémy's adrenalin spiked. Two men, one standing and one sitting. This one had been standing.

'You do remember.' The figure sounded pleased. 'The artist caught my best side, of course.'

It had been a *painting* he had seen that day, Rémy realized with a sudden rush of clarity. Old too, glowing with jewel-like colours. Two men... His stomach roiled. A small blue fan whirring at his feet flashed across his memory.

The figure floated closer. Malevolence emanated from him, hitting Rémy with pulsing, painful sound waves. He backed up against the railings beside his mother. The old balcony groaned.

'The pain in your head will subside soon, unless, of

course, you decide to be uncooperative. I have been searching for you for a very long time,' the man said.

He was wearing a red satin frock coat, its skirt brushing his knees, a white blouse with frilled cuffs and a stiff, ruffled collar open and cut low at his hairless chest. The man's androgyny would have been seductive, had it not been for the smooth white skin stretching across his high cheekbones that suggested puberty had never quite been reached. His breeches were close-fitting and his feet bare, flies crawling in and out of flesh where toenails had once been.

'What do you want?' croaked Rémy. 'Where's my aunt?'

The man flicked a manicured finger across a diamond stud in his ear. 'Your aunt is not your most immediate concern.'

Rémy noticed a handful of papers, covered in his mother's writing, gripped between the tapered thumb and little finger of the man's right hand. The hand was maimed, three stumps where there should have been fingers.

'Yes,' said the man, following his gaze. 'These papers are of great interest. But they don't contain what I need. You know what I'm talking about, I'm sure.'

Rémy didn't.

'You'll never get it, Don Grigori,' said Annie suddenly.

The flies swooped. Rémy cried out as his mother started singing again, holding the filthy creatures off with her voice.

Don Grigori fixed his eyes on her. 'Where have you put it?'

'Far away,' Annie choked. 'Where you'll never find it.'

The balcony groaned more loudly.

'Come inside, Mom,' Rémy begged. 'The balcony's going to break…'

The legion of bluebottles increased their buzzing.

'Your mother is being as stubborn as ever,' said Don Grigori irritably. 'Bring her inside, Rémy. Tell her she'll be safe. I just need a little information from her, and then you and I will take our leave.'

He put his palm flat against Rémy's chest, sending a frisson of electricity through his body. Rémy's hands twitched, his knees buckled and he felt himself getting erect. He slapped Don Grigori's hand away, horrified.

'I'm not going anywhere with you!'

'I hope you won't be as stubborn as your mother, now,' Don Grigori chided. 'Come, Annie. Tell me what I need to know and you will be amply rewarded.'

What did his mother have that this creature wanted so badly?

'Escort your mother inside, Rémy,' Don Grigori whispered. 'Let's help her… heal.'

# 18.

# WE ALL FALL DOWN

It was a long drop from the fourth floor to the ground below. The soundtrack of the neighbourhood – bus airbrakes exhaling at every stop, truck wheels walloping over potholes, police sirens bleating, car alarms wailing, a distant train horn – all faded to background noise. The air was still, the world holding its breath.

'Mom, we have to go inside,' Rémy said, pushing his mother gently in the back.

Annie kept singing, a Nina Simone song now, keeping Don Grigori at bay. The despair in her cracking voice made Rémy's skin tingle. She was dropping notes.

How long had she been out here?

A fault line in the balcony zigzagged beneath his feet. There was an expression of such defeat and disappointment, sorrow and love in his mother's eyes that he stepped back. He felt the balcony shift away from the railing.

'Find it, baby,' whispered his mother, so quietly Rémy almost missed it. 'I love you.'

She hugged him. Rémy felt something cool and hard slither down the neck of his tucked T-shirt, coming to rest against the skin at his waist.

Stepping back into the room, Annie opened her mouth and sang a top C.

The balcony split in two. Rémy fell, slamming on to the balcony directly beneath, the hard landing punching the air from his lungs. He fought for his next few breaths. He couldn't get air to fill his lungs. Pain pierced his shoulder, and he was covered in planks of softwood and pieces of rusty railing. He stared in disbelief up at what was left of the balcony above, the split wood like broken teeth. He could hear Don Grigori losing patience, shouting now.

'Tell me where the journal is!'

'Help her! She's going to fall,' sobbed Rémy, his ribs screaming in pain.

Don Grigori reached down with a slim, red-satin arm, lifted Annie up as easily as if she were a feather, and pulled her inside.

From beneath the broken balcony, Rémy heard his mom scream and Tia Rosa howl. A window exploded, raining shards of glass down on him.

## 19.

## TAKE THIS AND GO

Rémy clawed at the planks and pieces of railing. His shoulder was on fire, but he scrambled to his knees fast. He had to get back up there. He had to help.

'What the hell happened to you, Rem? What did you do to my balcony?'

Rémy looked up at Sotto Square's concerned face. In his late twenties, with light chocolate skin, Sotto had tats inked on most of his upper body and trouble etched in his face. On closer examination the tats were works of art, not prison ink. And every morning for as long as Rémy could remember, he would see Sotto on his balcony massaging baby oil into every one of them.

Sotto Square held sway with the gangs, the drug dealers and the pimps in this hood. Sotto was an urban entrepreneur, a thief and a scavenger, fencing stolen goods from the building's unused underground parking garages. His grandmother was the only tenant in the building who owned a car, a 1970s sea-green Lincoln that Sotto kept in immaculate condition and rarely drove.

There were no raiding parties on kids he knew, to use them as drug runners, and no selling to anyone in the building. Guns and weapons were left at the door. Like a knight, Sotto Square had a code of honour. Anyone who lived in his castle was family and earned his protection. In return, he expected fealty and a contribution to the building's upkeep in kind or cash. From a young age, Rémy had been responsible for mopping the hallways and mowing the lawns.

Sotto lived on the third floor of the building, his G'ma in the apartment next door on the right, and his cousin Two Square on the left. Rémy, Tia Rosa, his mom and G'ma would eat corndogs wrapped in crispy bacon and watch black-and-white horror movies on Sotto's massive flat screen well into the night, and on summer nights, G'ma insisted Rémy step on to her balcony and play taps on her old trumpet.

When Sotto's sister died in a drive-by outside her school, Rémy played his own arrangement of Eubie Blake's 'Memories of You' on G'ma's trumpet, bringing everyone to their feet. For one of the first times in his life, Rémy had a flash of awareness that something otherworldly permeated his playing.

Pulling Rémy up, Sotto glanced at the shattered balcony above. 'Looks like a war zone up there,' he remarked.

'You should go to the ER. I'll get the mess cleaned up and repaired. I can take care of the bill if you go to County.'

'Just got the wind knocked out of me. Nothing's broken,' said Rémy. 'I have to go, man, thanks...'

Sotto called out as Rémy limped towards the stairwell. 'Hey, Rem? Want a little somethin' take the edge off? On the house.'

The last thing Rémy needed right now was to dull his senses. The only way he was going to survive any of this was to keep his imagination alert.

A couple of bluebottles lay dying on the linoleum inside his apartment door. The table was still upturned and the room trashed. Tia Rosa was leaning over the sink, the water running, drinking from her cupped hand.

Rémy stared at the blood pooling at his aunt's feet. Tia Rosa glanced at him with fading eyes, a blackened knife in her hand.

'Stuck him like a pig,' she whispered. 'Shame he stuck me too. He won't be bothering you for a while. I promised Annie I would protect you...'

She smiled and slid to the floor.

'Shit, shit, shit...' His hands shaking, Rémy started to dial 911 when he heard footsteps. A distorted shadow stretched to the ceiling.

He dropped the phone.

His mom was bent over, pressing her hands against

a bloody wound in her lower abdomen as big as a man's fist. Bluebottle larvae were crawling in and out of her gut.

Rémy made an inarticulate sound of horror. He couldn't think, he had to *think*.

'You still have it, baby boy?' she whispered, as soft as a breeze.

Rémy remembered the cold thing she'd dropped down his neck on the balcony. He pulled it out: a brass key and a piece of a broken metal tablet carved with curious glyphs, on a worn leather strap.

His mother seemed to relax. 'Mailbox at Waterloo Station... Number... is on the key.'

'Waterloo Station? In *London*? Mom, hold on!' Rémy began to sob, rocking his mother's ruined body in his arms. 'Mom, please don't leave me. I don't want to be by myself...'

Two wet, bloody bluebottles fluttered from Annie's lips and crawled down her chin.

'Knew this day was coming ever since I saw him in the archives. I saw him step from a painting and try to take you, my baby boy... When I went back after... after... the accident, the painting was gone, I lost it... I lost it... Oh, I wished I'd had more time...'

'You gotta let me call 911, Mom. I can't just let you die—'

'You have to go, Rémy. Put... the tablet on, baby boy.'

Helplessly, Rémy slipped the segment of the etched tablet and the key around his neck. He felt the tablet vibrate against his skin, just a soft fluttering, but a vibration nonetheless.

'Do you feel it?'

Remy nodded.

'It'll get warmer when you get closer.'

'Closer to what?'

He sobbed. 'Closer to what? What am I looking for... Oh, Mom, don't go... please don't leave me.'

'Closer to...' Her lips were blue, her breathing shallow, laboured, painful. Rémy's tears were blinding him.

'RD, go. To London. Get... the journal. Find the Moor. He'll know... what to do.'

With her last breath, his mom reached across the kitchen floor and clasped Tia Rosa's dead hand.

# THIRD MOVEMENT

# 20.

# TIME TRAVEL SUCKS

'Time is running out, Matt,' Em said, nudging her brother over to make room at the end of the wooden jetty. Muted waves rippled on to the rocky shore beneath them.

'Go away, Em.' Matt paused before adding with considerable emphasis, 'I've not made my decision yet.'

'Matt, how is that even possible?' Em snapped back. 'Every other Animare has to make up their mind when they are sixteen. But the Council gave us both a whole extra year so that you could decide. If Lizzy's really not the one, then your final option for an official-by-the-scroll Guardian is me. And you know how everyone feels about that, including Zach.'

Matt glanced at the ridiculous expression on his twin sister's face. He knew she was thinking of Zach Butler's amazing body in skinny jeans. He could hear her in his mind. Dropping his sunglasses from the top of his head, he squinted in disgust at his sister.

Em grinned, punching him playfully on the shoulder. 'You must admit Zach and I are an Animare and Guardian dream team.'

'Can you stop talking now?' Matt said. He turned his face up to the morning sun, and dangled his feet in the wide ribbon of Largs Bay that separated their home in Auchinmurn from its smaller sister island, Era Mina.

Matt and Em had arrived on the islands when they were 12, fleeing London after they'd animated themselves into a Georges Seurat painting in the National Gallery. Their frantic arrival at the abbey's compound was the start of a dangerous journey that transported the twins to the island's medieval past and revealed they were part of an ancient order of artists known as Animare – powerful men and women who could bring their art to life. And because their dad had been a Guardian, the siblings had developed Guardian powers of inspiriting and mind-control.

'The Council of Guardians have made it clear that this union ceremony,' said Em, 'this joining together, is our last chance to be a legitimate part of the Animare world. Don't you want that?'

'Still talking,' said Matt.

'Mattie, our acceptance will open up opportunities I want to be part of! But you need a Guardian!'

Matt said nothing. He looked back at the house, a renovated monastery and its abbey, and at Renard, their grandfather and one of the most powerful Guardians in the world, standing at the open French doors. Matt could sense Renard's attention on them even while his eyes were observing the catering circus unfolding on the Abbey compound's expansive lawn.

Waiting staff darted in and out of a white canopy carrying champagne flutes, tea services and vases bursting with yellow blooms freshly cut from the garden. The ringmaster for the event was Jeannie Butler, the Abbey's elderly housekeeper and an Animare with unprecedented powers in her own right. Wrapped in a starched tartan pinnie, she stood in front of Renard on the stone steps of the patio and shouted instructions to a trio of tuxedoed musicians unpacking their instruments on a small stage nearby. No one skimped on a union ceremony.

'Do you remember when our feet couldn't touch the water from here?' Em asked, looking at her purple varnished toes hanging over the jetty, before splashing water on to Matt's cuffed jeans.

'Feels like another lifetime ago,' Matt said curtly. He didn't like talking about the past.

'Kind of was. Remember the day we arrived? We drew for Grandpa and accidentally animated a T-Rex on the hillside. Almost killed Zach.'

'Em—'

'OK. Zipped.' Em pinched her fingertips together, twisting them against her lips. She drew circles in the cool water with her toes.

*You know that Zach's afraid we're all going to wake up one morning and you'll just be gone.*

Matt shoved his shades back up into his long dark hair. 'Talking in my head is still talking.'

Apart from the scars on his arms and legs, the changes to Matt's dazzling, damaged eyes were the most visible signs of the time-travelling trauma he had suffered three years earlier.

'Zach's coming in,' Em said, sitting up and gazing out over the bay. 'He looks so hot on his board. Doesn't he?'

'You want me to lust after your boyfriend too?' Matt inquired.

Em watched Zach arch his body against his rig to catch the breeze from the Atlantic. May in Scotland was a chancy month: as much a chance of sun as of sleet, hail or high water. It was sunny now, and Zach had peeled his wetsuit off to his waist, his tanned body wet and muscular.

'Seriously hot,' she said happily.

'I'll go and bring him in,' said Matt, getting to his feet.

'No, you won't,' said Em, catching Matt's arm. 'The sun's too bright for your eyes.'

The physical transformation to Matt's eyes had begun two years ago, about six months after his return from the fourteenth century. At first, it was occasional blurred vision and then a painful sensitivity to bright sunlight. After a year, his eyes began to change colour from a brilliant cobalt to a cold, pale arctic blue. Then, just when he'd accepted the physical changes, fizzing lines like electric currents appeared in his peripheral vision, fluctuating with the light, framing everything Matt looked at with a pulsing halo.

The winter following the twins' sixteenth birthday, Matt woke up swearing his eyeballs were melting. When his mother managed to coax Matt to open them, it was as if he was staring at the world from under murky water. A translucent film like an alligator's third eyelid had dropped over his eyeballs.

For three days Matt stayed in his room, alternating cold compresses with warm poultices of Jeannie's concoction. The poultices looked like sanitary pads soaked in pea soup. As if that wasn't bad enough, Matt was convinced she had lathered the poultice in sheep's dung too. But it seemed to work, giving him a modicum of relief from the burning, and after a while he developed a tolerance to the smell. The other advantage the poultice had was in keeping Em and Zach at a tolerable distance, so Matt did not have to witness their far-too-frequent bouts of snogging.

One morning after a restless night, Matt's eyes had itched more than they throbbed. In the bathroom, he'd drenched his eyes with a warm face cloth until Jeannie's crusty mixture loosened from his eyelids, then leaned his head over the sink and wiped the final layer of sludge from his eyes.

Em had tapped gently on the door. 'Are you OK? Your anxiety is making my stomach ache.'

Throwing a towel over his head, Matt had opened the door. 'Something's changed,' he said.

'What?'

'I haven't looked.'

Em had rolled her eyes. 'You'd better look now!'

'But what if I can't see anything? My eyes are itching like crazy.'

'Oh, for… put on your big-boy pants. Besides, itching's usually a sign of healing.' Em had softened her tone. 'Do you want me to look first?'

Matt had sighed. 'Let's look together. Turn off the light first. I have a feeling it's gonna hurt.'

Em had hit the switch, plunging the room into semi-darkness, and Matt took off the towel, keeping his eyes closed.

'How bad do I look?' he'd asked anxiously.

'Your skin's pretty red, but that's probably from rubbing off Jeannie's poultice like a crazy person.' Setting her hands on Matt's shoulders, Em had tried to inspirit and calm him. 'Ready?' she said.

As Matt slowly opened his eyes, his relief had flowed through Em's palms.

'Thank God,' he said. 'You're just as ugly as ever.'

Em had whacked him. 'I knew you would be able to see— oh my God, wow!'

Matt froze. 'What?'

'Your irises are huge, with slivers of light floating in them. Looks like you've had drops put in your eyes... or you've been smoking... Have you been smoking?'

'It's six in the morning!'

'Take a look. It's super cool, in a Prince-of-the-Damned kinda way.'

Matt had faced his reflection. The whites of his eyes were almost non-existent. 'Jesus. I look like I'm possessed.'

'It is a wee bit creepy, I can't deny. How many fingers am I holding up?' Em had said, waving her middle finger in front of Matt's face.

Matt had gently slapped her hand away, then grabbed a hair band and pulled his hair into a ponytail before examining himself more carefully. He was paler than usual, but other than eyes like dark blue marbles flecked with light, he'd looked OK. And when he gazed around the bathroom, everything seemed normal.

'I'm... I think I'm good.'

Em had jumped from the counter, knocking Zach's contact container and solution on to the floor. Forgetting Matt's earlier discomfort, she'd flipped on the bathroom light.

Matt had been plunged into darkness. He'd dropped to his knees, the heels of his hands pressed against his eyes, his agonized howls bringing the entire Abbey into the bathroom.

Now, his vision was only unimpaired in complete darkness. He could see as keenly in the dark as any night predator. As a result he'd become a night owl, a kind of vampire, wandering around the Abbey alone until the small hours, and, on most occasions, sleeping well into the day.

He wore shades most of the time. They helped keep the flashing images at bay. They also stopped people staring at him. But the one compensation for Matt's distorted vision was how shockingly, disturbingly beautiful his eyes had become. Em had no doubt that one inspiriting look from Matt's eyes could easily bring Lord Nelson down from atop his column.

# 21.

# OUTSIDE THE HIGH KIRK

Despite all the weird alchemy happening to Matt's vision, the most surreal transformation occurred a month later. The twins and Zach were at the end of a day trip to Edinburgh. With an hour to spare before their return train to Largs, Em insisted the three of them check out a stained-glass window at the High Kirk, recently restored and glowing with colour.

After five minutes, Matt and Zach went to perch on the bollards outside.

'Pretty much what I expected,' signed Zach. 'Coloured glass. Lots of it.'

Matt shrugged. 'Em operates on a different universe of enthusiasm from most people.'

Two girls slowed to a stroll and stopped at the foot of the statue of Adam Smith, glancing at Matt and Zach with obvious interest. Matt rubbed his eyes. A headache had been taunting him all day. The overcast Edinburgh sky wasn't helping.

He suddenly felt as if an opaque screen had slipped over his eyes, filtering out colour and light. Like a drunk, he wobbled off the bollard and fell on to the cobbles. For a horrible second he was in complete darkness.

Then a shrieking woman with no front teeth began smacking him repeatedly across the side of the head with a scuffed leather book. Instinctively covering his head with his arms, Matt scrambled to his feet and stared in shock at the mob of women surrounding him on the steps of the kirk. Every one of them looked as if they were cosplaying Downton Abbey kitchen maids. And they were all locked in what appeared to be hand-to-hand combat with a battalion of tin solders come to life.

'Get aff me, ye bastard! Fore I beat the devil out of ye,' screamed one of the women as a soldier grabbed her shoulders and threw her to the ground.

More than a little confused, Matt ducked, only to be thumped in the chest by a stool flying from the hands of a young woman with a filthy apron and spiky hair.

'I'll no be told by anyone what to say to my God!'

The women charged at the soldiers. Matt pivoted in a split second to avoid the clash. 'What the—'.

'In the name of God, ladies, stop this affront! Yer no animals! Put down your stools!' yelled a man in a black frock coat with a white collar, loose at his neck.

The minister tried to speak again, but before the words escaped his lips, the woman with the spiky hair threw a heavy punch to his jaw, knocking him to the ground at the bottom of the church steps. Three other women whaled on him with stools. Matt found he couldn't just stand there and watch. Diving into the fray, he grabbed the minister by the collar to drag him loose. At once he was rounded on by one of the attackers.

'Get off me, you crazy woman!'

A rotten cabbage flew towards Matt's head and he rolled on to the street… into the path of an oncoming cyclist.

The cyclist swerved and swore. 'Take yer drinking inside, ya stupit bastard!'

Matt was dimly aware of Zach and Em rushing towards him.

'Matt, what are you doing? Do you have some kind of death wish?'

Matt was having trouble focusing on the peaceful square. Where had the fight gone?

'The women were attacking me,' he managed.

Em zoned in on the two girls by the statue goggling at Matt. 'Them?' she said. 'Why would they attack you?'

Matt let Zach help him to his feet. 'Not them,' he said helplessly. 'The other women… The ones with…' He tried to gesture 'stools' and 'aprons' but it wasn't coming out right.

Em stared at him.

'We need to go home,' she said. 'And talk.'

*

Twenty minutes after Matt's skirmish, his eyes still hadn't stopped watering, the sparking lights around the edges of his vision more insistent than ever. He had a headache sharp enough to crack an egg and the caffeine in the two Red Bulls he'd gulped wasn't helping dull the pain.

'Tell,' Em commanded as the train pulled out of Waverley Station.

'Don't laugh,' said Matt finally, 'but I just experienced some kind of flashback outside St Giles.'

Minutes into Matt's description of the fight scene, Em was Googling his description. With a snort of triumph, she passed her phone to Matt. Matt stared at a picture of a mob of women throwing stools and prayer books at soldiers in front of St Giles.

'But… that's it,' he said in astonishment.

Em read the caption. 'It's a woodcut depicting a riot during the Bishops' Wars that resulted in the signing of the National Covenant in 1638.'

Zach and Matt both looked blank.

'The National Covenant,' said Em, 'was one of the first political documents proclaiming people had a right to worship what and how they wanted.' She looked at her brother with awe. 'You just witnessed a major historical event. Do you know how crazy that is?'

'Whatever I witnessed,' Matt said with feeling, 'I'd be OK with not witnessing it again.'

'We should tell Mum,' said Em.

Matt fixed his sister with his best death stare. 'Don't you dare.'

'I think it's cool.' Zach's signing was more animated than it had been for a while. 'A new angle on your abilities.'

'Easy for you to say.' Matt winced at the bruise flowering on his spine. 'You don't have a three-legged stool imprinted on your back.'

Although Em had never experienced a visual flashback like Matt, her abilities were developing in their own way.

A few months earlier, she had been in Edinburgh with her mum, shopping. As they wandered in the Grassmarket and turned into a vaulted passageway to an antique store, Em had been violently sick without warning. No time for cupping her hands to her mouth, or grabbing a tissue, or even rushing to the gutter – just a sudden wave of revulsion and then a projectile of vomit on to the stone steps. A couple of tourists travelling in the opposite direction stopped, eyes wide in horror, then backed away.

Em's pulse was racing. Her stomach felt like jelly, but the nausea had gone by the time she and her mother had sat themselves at a nearby café, where Sandie bought two bottles of water and a Mars bar.

'Whoa,' said Em, sipping the water. 'I don't know what just happened.'

'Em,' Sandie began, 'I know that you and Zach are close. Really close.' She cleared her throat. 'And I... well... do you think...'

Em almost spat the water out. 'Mum! Awkward. I'm not pregnant!'

Sandie leaned back on the chair, exhaling audibly. 'OK, OK. But you know if you are, you know, having sex, I hope you're—'

'Mum, stop,' said Em, wincing. 'I know. Birth control. Protection. Got it. It's Lecture Number Four.'

Sandie looked horrified. 'You've numbered my... my advice? What's Number One?'

'Depends. My Number One, or Matt and Zach's?'

'Good God, you've even categorized them.' Sandie bit off a chunk of the chocolate bar. 'OK. Give me your Number One.'

'Boys always want to touch what they don't have,' Em said, mimicking Sandie's serious voice. The one she usually heard before going out in Seaport on a Saturday night.

Sandie burst into laughter.

'Well, it's true. You can thank my mother for that. That was her only contribution to my sex education. So, if you're not pregnant—'

'Muuum!'

'—then maybe it has something to do with your abilities? No one is sick like that for no reason.'

Later that evening, they had done a little research in

the Guardian archives, delving into Edinburgh's general history. They learned that many of the passageways, or pends, in Old Town had been restored using cobbles from where the Old Tollbooth had once stood: a place where witches and sorcerers were tortured and killed in the eighteenth century.

It looked like Em and Matt's burgeoning talents were continuing to complement each other. While Matt might *see* events *in situ*, Em *sensed* them, as if the places themselves spoke to her. She and her brother were still a team.

The thought comforted her more than she could say.

## 22

# MOTHBALLS AND LILACS

Matt watched with mixed emotions as Em and Zach kissed on the jetty. The Union Ceremony to be held in a couple of hours may not have been marriage, but it was just as binding. Every Animare was partnered with a Guardian for life, to protect and inspire the Animare and his or her art. For the conservative members on the Council of Guardians, the relationship was also meant to keep the Animare in check, to make sure he or she did not bring attention to their existence in the world. He couldn't shake the absurdity of choosing not only your future path at seventeen, but also the person who'd accompany you on that journey. It was medieval.

How could anyone go through with it?

Leaving them, he trudged up the garden, past the waiters and the tent, the tables and chairs, all the way up to his room. Lying on his bed, he shoved his face into his pillow. He loved his family. He did. But they'd never understand what had happened to him when he was lost in the past.

*Thanks for the only gift you gave me, Dad. Self-awareness.*

There was a knock at his door.

'Simon's seating the Council in the library,' Lizzy said, poking her head into Matt's room. Her Guardian robe suited her, her long blonde hair in a fancy updo. 'Em and Zach are already downstairs. We've about five minutes before they begin without us.'

She held out a heavy brocade robe to Matt.

'Put it on then,' she said as Matt hesitated. 'Come on, I'll help.'

She lifted the robe on to Matt's shoulders, straightening the material against his back, running her fingers over its intricate stitching and its detailed design. She turned him to face the mirror.

Matt's eyes had trouble filtering his reflection. He blinked rapidly, letting the kaleidoscope of colours in his pupils settle. The robe was a lush burgundy and hung loose, in thick pleats of material, on his lithe frame. Silver threads, stitched in an overlapping infinity design, were piped around the cuffs of the wide sleeves and streamed down the floor-length lapels, the robe's silver clasps shaped like the claws of a beast. The collar was stiff and high, framing his sharp features and keeping his long hair curled against the pale skin of his neck. The garment was lined in ermine that smelled to Matt of mothballs and lilacs. He turned to view the back. Embroidered in shimmering threads of silver was a flying stag, the peryton, and the symbol of the ancient order of Era Mina, to which he was about to belong.

'I look like Dumbledore's scary nephew.'

'Lose the Ray-Bans,' suggested Lizzy. 'The room will be lit by candles and all the windows in the library have been draped. You shouldn't need them.'

Matt slipped off his shades and handed them over.

'Better,' Lizzy said. 'Now you look like Snape, who I always thought was kinda sexy.'

Lizzy's boldness made Matt nervous. 'I probably should've cut my hair,' he mumbled.

Em and Zach were waiting in the foyer. Like Lizzy's, Zach's robe was lighter in colour but adorned with the same intricate glyphs and elegant stitching as the robes the twins were wearing.

'Glad to see you look about as stupid as I feel,' signed Zach to Matt.

'No,' Matt signed back, grinning despite his unease, 'Pretty sure Em looks more ridiculous than any of us.'

'I aim to please,' said Em.

Sandie squeezed Lizzy's arm and then Zach's before crossing the foyer to embrace her children. 'You look so grown-up,' she sighed. 'I'm so proud of both of you. These past few years have been rough, but you've demonstrated more strength of character than most adults would've done in similar positions.'

An elderly Guardian, in a scarlet robe trimmed in gold ermine, tapped lightly on the foyer floor with a ceremonial staff. 'Ladies and gentlemen, we are ready to begin.'

Zach shifted directly behind Lizzy and Em stepped behind Matt.

*Whatever you do, Mattie, I'll support you.*

Matt felt such a rush of love and joy from Em's touch, as pure as anything he'd ever felt before, that he swallowed a gasp.

Impatiently, the piper was repeating the processional for the third time.

*That's our cue, Matt. C'mon.*

Matt grinned when he saw how his mum had lit the elegant Victorian library. Specimen jars filled with glowing jellyfish, the kind that clogged the bay between Largs and Auchinmurn, stood on the bookshelves, casting a lustrous blue light on the chairs and dais. The glass cabinets, containing the library's priceless manuscripts, had been draped with silver gauze to eliminate glare. The room looked like a scene from a medieval coronation arranged by Salvador Dali and Edgar Allen Poe: enchanting with a big dash of the macabre.

*Looks like one of your sketches, Em.*

*Right? I love it. We should keep it this way.*

As the piper concluded and stepped aside, the four inductees walked down the aisle to where Renard, their grandfather, and Jeannie, their beloved housekeeper, stood in their ceremonial robes. They took the empty seats in front of Simon, Zach's dad, and their mom, Sandie. Vaughn's seat was empty. Matt wondered where he was.

'*Fáilte go dtí ceann amháin agus go léir!*' said Renard in a booming voice.

'Welcome! Council members, dear friends and close family. It's customary to open this special ceremony with the "Oath of the Council of Guardians" read by the order's historian, Simon Butler.'

Before opening the first folio of the ancient illustrated codex known to members as 'Albion's Book of Days', Simon slipped on a pair of cotton gloves to protect the priceless parchment from the oils on his skin. The Guardians in the library, including Matt and Em, felt a low-pitched hum from the codex like a song's heavy bass-line vibrating in your chest.

'With honour and loyalty,' Simon began, 'we, the Council of Guardians of the Order of Era Mina, pledge to uphold the rules of our ancient guild, to foster the varied ambitions, nurture the powerful creativity and support the awe and wonder of all Animare under our care.'

'With honour and loyalty, we pledge to protect their art and their lives from any who would dare bring harm,' recited the assembled Guardians. '*Is mac-mean-mna màthair cumhachd…* imagination is the real and the eternal, the mother of all power.'

Renard and Jeannie's robes were covered in hundreds of tiny glorious glyphs. For Matt, the embroidery was a three-dimensional display of colours and shapes, full-blown animations dancing up from the fabric as if the Animare who'd created the robes had stitched the fates, good and bad, of their brothers and sisters into the cloth. Every few seconds, the figures on the robes shifted positions, as if each image was trying to take its turn in reality. On Renard's shoulder, a medieval monk rose up, only to be cut down by a knight wielding a broadsword, his horse's hooves stitched fast to the cloth with golden threads. The monk's blood was sucked into the fabric of the robe before bursting into flames, the monk's black flesh falling in charred drops around Renard's elbow.

Jeannie's robe was alive too, monsters and men shifting shapes, morphing colours in a tableau of the fantastic and the grotesque, a violent melee of torture and triumph.

*Can you see the images on the robes animate, Mattie?*
*I wish I couldn't.*

Em looked pale. *I think we're seeing all the ways the monks at Era Mina were tortured and killed. Do you think Renard and Jeannie can feel what they're wearing?*

Matt concentrated on the emotions of the two people he loved most in the world. *They can feel them. It's like they're wearing hair shirts.*

*Then why wear them?*

*Masochism? Or tradition.*

Em bit her lip. *No matter the suffering?*

*This is what we're signing up for*, Matt thought to himself. He closed his eyes, shutting away the ceremony, the robes and his sister.

Em suddenly felt as if a claw was squeezing the breath from her lungs. One or two Guardians shot to their feet. Others fainted and toppled to the floor. The specimen jars exploded one after the other, sending shards of glass and blobs of jellyfish raining down on the gathering.

Matt's face was pinched. He snatched his shades from Lizzy's hand and stepped up to the podium.

'I'm sorry, everyone,' he said. 'I can't do this. It has nothing to do with you, Lizzy, or you either, Em. This is all on me. And I hope one day you'll all be able to forgive me.'

He unhooked his robe and slipped it off. Mutters of shock and concern spread through the room. The last time an Animare and a Guardian had failed to go forward with a Union Ceremony was at the turn of the century, when John Singer Sergeant's Guardian dropped dead from a brain aneurysm during the ceremony itself. As far as anyone knew, no one had ever not gone through with it of his or her own volition.

Renard raised his hand in the air, calming the commotion.

'Matt's decision may be unprecedented, but as far as I know it is not against the rules of our order. It is clear that he didn't make it lightly. But Matt,' he said, addressing his grandson directly, 'you must understand that there may be consequences imposed by the Council. Consequences I cannot save you from.'

Matt looked at Em. He could sense nothing from her. It worried him more than everyone else's responses put together.

Renard shuffled his notes on the podium and cleared his throat before speaking again.

'So if I may ask you all to settle your hearts and your imaginations, I'd like to continue the ceremony with Emily Calder and Zach Butler.'

Zach leaped from his chair so fast he knocked it over.

'Easy does it, son,' Simon remarked. Laughter cut through some of the tension.

Em stayed where she was. Em, who was crying. Em who never cried. Matt's heart clenched, then leaped with hope.

'Em?' said Zach.

## 23.

# BANKSY AND MERLIN

Two days later, the twins exploded from Johannes Vermeer's *The Allegory of Painting* in waves of greys and greens. Matt stumbled a little, but fought the momentum, skidding to a stop against an upholstered chair where someone had been reading old newspapers. Clippings from neat piles stacked on the chair's arms flurried at Matt's feet.

Em wasn't as graceful, crashing out of the Vermeer on a slick of viscous paint. Punching into reality, arms akimbo, legs splayed, she thudded into a draughtsman's table, knocking a cup of pens and brushes on to the floor, her hip slamming against the corner of the table, before landing on her bum under the desk.

'OK?' asked Matt.

'Nah,' Em quipped, gasping. 'Fractured hip.'

The last two days had been exhausting, stacked on top of several levels of awkward. Em knew she'd made the right decision to stick with Matt, but her heart still ached.

Zach's anger and misery had been so acute he had barely signed a word to her, cutting her off from his thoughts entirely. When she tried to access his mind, he imagined a computer firewall, so all Em could see were lines and lines of computer code. When Em had tried to breach his defences one last time before they'd left, the code had spelled out, 'Fuck off.'

Em really hoped Jeannie was right, and time would heal his hurt. Em wasn't sure she was strong enough to carry Zach's rage like a boulder in her gut for very long.

The Vermeer still had a cyclone of colour and light swirling at its core, expanding beyond the border of its gilded frame as if it were about to burst free. It was so bright and rotating so fast that Em wondered if it might be strong enough to pull her back inside.

Vaughn Grant didn't so much drop as glide from the painting in one elegant movement. Colour and light from the painting stretched out behind him in a cape of blues, yellows and greens. When he was fully in the room, the painting shrugged back to its original state, only the faint telltale glow left as evidence.

Vaughn grinned and winked at Em, brushing flakes of blue paint from his jacket.

'Show off,' said Em, realizing that they were in a church.

'Welcome to Orion,' he said. 'We are essentially the MI6 of the Animare world, and you and Matt are our newest and youngest recruits. I hope you appreciate the strings I pulled to make this happen. God knows, the Council didn't know what to do with you after you rejected your chosen Guardians.'

The twins looked around at the space, the medieval pitched ceiling with its thick beams and the altar at the east end of the building. The ground was uneven and cobbled, marked every few metres with flagstones that had the names of the dead etched on them. Rows of canvases leaned against the walls next to blocks of marble in various states of reveal. Busts on pedestals sat beside empty gilded frames. The most amazing area in the church was a series of what looked to Em like Plexiglas coffins standing beneath a row of dusty skylights. Inside were concrete blocks cut from walls with graffiti on them, pictures of telephone boxes, police constables, doors and children.

Matt's expression changed. 'Whoah! Are those Banksys? Is he an Animare?'

'They are, and, yes, he is.'

Vaughn stepped round clusters of desks, some with massive computer screens on them, others piled with books, and light-tables for the close examination of paintings.

'One of our founders, James McIntosh Patrick, came upon this church and its surrounding land when he was on a scouting tour for his own landscapes. It was close to ruin. He bought it, renovated it and converted it to our Scottish headquarters. He was not a religious man, and appreciated the irony that Orion, where art is worshipped and imaginations revered, exists on a site reserved for God. It's also remote enough that our fading goes undetected.'

Em gazed at the stunning painting of the Saint-Martin Canal in Paris, on the wall opposite. It was by Alfred Sisley, an impressionist Animare along with Manet and Pissarro.

'Were all these paintings created for fading?' she asked.

'Only those two and a Turner over in the north transept,' Vaughn answered, 'but Orion has co-opted a few around the world and added paintings within those paintings, allowing us to fade more directly to and from places. We used to have to fade between art museums and galleries. This works better.'

'Not every Animare can fade, right?' Matt asked.

'No. We don't have much record of anyone fading, before the Renaissance,' Vaughn said. 'But that doesn't mean earlier Animare couldn't do it. It just means no one documented it. The problem with being a secret order is how little gets written down. Simon does his best these days, but…'

Regret and sadness stung Em's mind at the mention of Zach's dad. She wandered across the nave, giving herself a chance to get her emotions in check and force thoughts of Zach to the back of her mind. The altar looked like a throne built into the granite, a small, carved chalice jutting from the wall beside it.

'How old was the original chapel?' she asked, leaning forward to touch the smooth surface of the altar.

'Don't!' Vaughn said sharply. Em jumped away. 'I don't mean to scare you, but sometimes when a powerful Guardian touches this stone, he or she gets quite a shock. Not just a little spark, but a full-blown knockout.'

'Why?'

'We think Merlin was baptized on it.'

'King Arthur's Merlin?'

'Move away from the stone, Em,' Matt warned. 'We're not ready to meet a wizard today.'

'You can sleep down here, Matt,' Vaughn said, sorting through messages on his phone. 'Em, you can have the bed in the living quarters upstairs. I'll take the couch up there. I'll turn on the generator and get the place warmed up a bit. We're not on the grid.'

He pointed to an arched doorway in the medieval church wall. 'Our generator is at the bottom of the garden in a shed. There's a bathroom and small kitchen in there. Make yourselves at home.'

'This is trippy,' said Matt. 'Who else knows about this place?'

'Only Orion agents and members of the five Councils of Guardians. Each Council supports a similar site in its own territory.'

Matt lifted his shades off his eyes. 'At least it's dark in here.'

'It's always dark at this time of the day. Most natural light comes from the skylights on the roof, except for the diffused lights at the light-tables. We can't afford anyone to see our comings and goings. At the height of the day, you'll need your shades.'

'How many people work here?' asked Matt.

'Counting both of you? Four of us.'

Em walked the perimeter. She knew better than to touch the art. 'Four? That's a card game or a small dinner party, not a secret organization designed to protect Animare and their Guardians.'

'We manage just fine.'

'What about tourists visiting the church?'

'We don't get any. We're too far from the station and the nearest pub is ten miles away. Now get some kip. You both look bushed.'

Later, when Em was sure Matt and Vaughn were asleep, she pulled on her boots, grabbed her coat and went outside. The night was quieter than any night on Auchinmurn. No sounds of the sea. No squeals of the gulls. Even the moon looked different from here.

Using her phone as a flashlight, she walked along a pebbled path towards a bench under a copse of trees. The plaque dedicated the bench and its spot to the original sixth-century church, supposedly founded by St Kentigern. She tapped Zach's number. The call went straight to Zach's voicemail message, which he had tailored for her.

'Em, leave me alone. Stop calling.'

Em curled up on the hard bench, her loss and her anguish so profound that it woke Matt from the best night's sleep he'd had in ages.

# 24.

# MIDNIGHT IN PARIS

PRESENT DAY

M att and Em hugged the shadows of the Louvre's façade as they jogged towards an arched opening, midway down the side of the building. With his perfect night vision Matt was in the lead.

He held up his hand, stopping Em. 'Did you hear that? Behind us?'

Em listened. 'It's just traffic.' At the fourth arch from the bridge, they ducked into a small cobbled alley and jogged down a set of stone steps to a tiny forecourt in one of the oldest parts of the Louvre. The twins were engulfed in complete darkness, not even the Paris moon offering illumination.

'I can't see a thing,' said Em. 'And Georges is late.'

'We'll do it the old-fashioned way,' said Matt, 'I can see fine!'

Slipping his bulging sketchbook from inside his jacket, he untied the leather strips holding it together. He flipped to a page about two-thirds of the way in, to an image of a key, the kind used to open old doors and treasure chests. He stared at the key before outlining it quickly, slowing only to shade and contour the teeth. The edges of the drawing began to glow, pale at first then brighter and brighter. Seconds later the key fell from the page and clunked on to the stones at Em's feet. The light from the key lit up a small door cut into the wall in front of them. Em slipped the key in the lock, but stopped as a guard turned into the archway.

'Monsieur Matt? Mademoiselle Emily?'

Em felt light-headed with relief. 'We started without you, Georges.'

'*Desolé*. I saw you both on the bridge when I crossed the gardens.'

'We appreciate you didn't call the Council about this,' said Matt. 'Gives us a chance to clean up our mess.'

As Matt and the guard fiddled with a set of real keys to the medieval keep that loomed in the centre of the second courtyard, Em's imagination stirred. She could hear the gunshots, the shouts, the screams, the call to arms from the wooden barricade on the Rue de Six. She smelled gunpowder choking the air, mingling with the fires raging all over the city and the stench of blood flowing along the gutters and into the Seine in a great red ribbon of death.

During the bloodiest days of the French Revolution, four people had docked their boats against the nearby city wall, dislodged the main sewer grate that drained from the palace, climbed inside, and crawled in the pitch-black until they were directly beneath the spot where Em now stood. History wasn't clear on the details of what happened next, but they had somehow broken in, opened the sealed door to the medieval keep, exposesd the ancient tunnels that led into the Petite Galerie of the palace as it lay under siege, then hauled and hidden as many works of art as they could in the catacombs beneath the foundations. The only possible answer to the puzzle was that they had been Animare, and had animated keys in exactly the same way as Matt had done. That night they had saved centuries of art.

'This is as far as I can go,' said Georges. 'I must continue with my security checks.' He handed them a secure key card. 'This should get you where you need to go.'

'We'll try not to use the card unless we have to,' Matt said.

The guard nodded, relaxing a little. 'You will have approximately three minutes in any gallery before your body heat will trigger the alarms. It is the time it takes for a guard to move through each space. *Bonne chance.*'

Matt waited until the guard closed the keep's heavy door, before lifting the concealed trapdoor. He led Em down the iron steps and along a damp tunnel to an elevator shaft filled with concrete, blocked off by the Nazis during their occupation of the city. Once again,

Matt slipped his sketchbook and a nubby stick of charcoal from his inside pocket. As he drew, his fingers and charcoal were like pencils of light on the paper. As he sketched, the concrete cracked, crumbled and resolved itself into steps, spiralling upwards.

The twins took the stairs, two at a time, up to another set of elevator doors at the back of a storage room long since abandoned. Em pried the doors open as Matt tore up his drawing, letting the pieces flutter away as concrete filled in the stairs and closed off the shaft.

The room was filled with wall-to-wall packing crates. Matt popped the lid on the first two, sending a family of mice scuttling across the floor. In the third crate, he found what Georges had discovered.

The crate was the size of a coffin, and inside was an embroidered glowing animated pillow, along with a long pipe and a leather pouch filled with tobacco.

Em picked up the pouch and sniffed. 'It's him.'

On the other side of the door to the storage room, Em heard footsteps again. She flicked off the light and stepped behind the door, waiting. Matt backed against the wall next to her. A stray mouse darted round Em's feet and scampered under the door.

The footsteps stopped. The twins held their breath.

Then they heard their quarry sprinting in the other direction.

'Not again,' said Matt, yanking the door open.

# 25.

# NOT MY FAULT

The twins chased a man wearing a loose white tunic, leather breeches and a sword down the emergency stairs to the Louvre's main gallery. Sprinting down the marble steps, Matt clipped the edge of Winged Victory's bow-shaped plinth with his wrist. By the time he had stopped yelping at the pain, their prey had gone.

'If he gets into another painting, Vaughn'll have our hides,' said Em as Matt shook the feeling back into his wrist and hand.

Matt groaned. 'We should have trusted our instincts the first time,'

'Ha! You mean, you shouldn't have let your hormones run amok and flirted with him so shamelessly. He may be great to look at but he's dangerous.' Em jabbed the air above Matt with her finger. 'You knew two months ago when Vaughn gave us our first case.'

Matt flushed and pulled out his sketchbook.

'Whatever. We should have bound him like Vaughn

121

told us to, even if his information was good. How are we going to find him now? As sources go, he's a pain in the—'

Em pulled Matt's sketchbook from his hands and began to draw, glancing from Matt to Titian's nearby painting of the Angel Gabriel and back again.

Matt's eyes widened. 'Don't do this to me, Em…'

'This mess is not my fault,' Em reminded him tartly. Using the heel of her hands, she smudged the drawing, creating the texture of feathers.

A golden glow washed out from the painting and enveloped Matt. He dropped to his knees, his jacket ripping from his shoulders as if he was the Hulk, his eyes tearing with pain for the second time in as many minutes.

Em kneeled beside him. 'I didn't think it would hurt that much, Mattie. I'm sorry. But it's the best way we have of catching him, OK? Try to stand. We've only about two minutes left.'

Matt stood, wobbled, and dropped to his knees again. His centre of gravity was off. Em rubbed out a line here, one there, and thickened some shading in the background of the drawing. This time when Matt stood up, although the crushing weight on his back felt like he was carrying someone on his shoulders wrapped in barbed wire, he was mobile at least.

He opened and closed Titian's wings. The air rushed across Em's face. 'Go!' she shouted.

Matt jumped.

At first he thought he would face-plant into the marble, but then he found his balance and soared. He glided between the statues and down the long hallway to the European wing, exulting in the feeling. In a matter of seconds, he was crash-landing on top of the man in the tunic, knocking his sword from his hand.

'And so we meet again,' grinned the man, catching his breath. 'Gods preserve me!'

'They gave up on you a long time ago, Caravaggio. This is for these bloody wings.' Matt punched him in the nose.

## 26.

# OLD FRIENDS

With as much grace as he could muster, Matt folded his wings against his back and stood up. 'That was uncalled for,' Caravaggio complained, cupping his bloody nose.

'You shouldn't have run off last time then, should you?' Matt's wings were heavy and reeked of oil and aniseed. Under his shirt, blood trickled from beneath his shoulder blades where the wings had burst through his skin. He kicked the sword out of Caravaggio's reach.

The artist's eyes glinted. 'Are we going to play a game again?'

'I'm tired of playing games with you, man,' said Matt. 'You promised us, no more jumping into the world from your art. We can't keep covering for your actions. Sooner or later someone other than a well-bribed guard will notice your comings and goings, and when that happens we will all be bound for good.'

'The information I gave Orion about that animation in Venice paid dividends, did it not?'

Matt had to admit, Vaughn had been impressed with the way he and Em had dealt with the Venice mission, their first one. But Caravaggio's fondness for a fight had made him a little too visible in Venice, and Vaughn had tasked the twins with catching him and bringing him into Orion's HQ. It was proving harder than expected. The last time they had met, Caravaggio charmed Matt a little too much and Matt had let him – against Em's better judgement. If it happened again, Matt could only imagine what Vaughn would say.

'I don't see why I can't remain your little secret,' Caravaggio said, grinning at Matt. 'We could be very good together. I'm quite sure I can be helpful again.'

Caravaggio combed his shaggy brown hair from his eyes with his fingers, and attempted to sneak a small step towards his sword. Matt was quicker, grabbing the artist's arm and twisting him to the ground, crashing him against a plinth displaying a naked statue of Bacchus. Caravaggio lifted his eyes at the statue's glory hanging directly above his head, then winked at Matt.

Matt couldn't help himself. He cracked up.

'Will you two get a grip?' Em said, running breathlessly down the corridor towards them. 'We have one minute, and counting!'

'Stay put,' said Matt, trying hard not to admire the man's flair. In his tight breeches and a tunic open in a long V at his chest, Caravaggio looked every part the rake that history depicted. Matt could well believe the stories he'd heard about the artist's love affairs. Like the story of the time he'd been rustled in the night from a countess's bed, only to sneak along the gilded hallway to enter the chambers of the count later.

*For God's sake, stop lusting after him, Mattie. That's what got us in trouble the last time.*

'Let me go,' said Caravaggio. 'I have not caught the villain who slew my lover and laid the blame at my feet. How is it fair that I should remain a wanted man for all time for a murder I did not commit?'

'No one cares about a murder that happened 400 years ago,' Matt said.

Caravaggio pouted. 'I have not been hiding in my own paintings for 400 years to be denied now. And I'm close, I know it. There is a painting at Les Invalides—'

'Thirty seconds,' Em said helplessly.

'I would be happy to accompany you from this place,' said Caravaggio, pulling himself to his feet. 'In return for my freedom, I have fresh information of vital importance to Orion. The Camarilla is back.'

'Who?' Em asked.

'Let me go and I will tell you more. You will not find them by yourselves. They are too good at hiding in the shadows.' Caravaggio looked smug. 'But I am a master of shadows, as any critic will tell you, and they cannot hide from me. My genius is a heavy burden to bear.'

'You're a heavy burden to bear,' said Matt, checking his phone. 'Where's the closest painting for fading, Em?'

'Somewhere in the European wing. We need to split up. We'll find the painting faster. Can you handle him alone?'

'Go.'

Em darted up the stairs and out to another wing. Caravaggio took advantage of the moment, kicking his sword up from the ground and into his hands in one fluid moment.

'You're too easily distracted, dear boy.'

Matt sidestepped, avoiding Caravaggio's sword by millimetres.

'We should make these meetings a regular event,' said Caravaggio, lunging at Matt again.

Matt darted backwards. 'Seriously, we're doing this here? And now?'

'I cannot have you and your sister taking me in. You know the Councils will vote to have me bound back in one of my paintings, this time forever, and I hate to leave unfinished business.'

Caravaggio's footwork and sword skills were far superior to Matt's sidestepping.

'Or Em and I could just bind you ourselves,' said Matt, ducking. 'We're strong enough. No one would ever know.'

'I don't want to hurt you, my friend.' Caravaggio sighed, slicing across the arm of Matt's jacket before pivoting and tearing a gash in Matt's jeans. 'All I ask is you forget you ran into me here. Let me take care of my business and disappear as I planned.'

Matt tackled the artist, charging into his legs, taking them both down. Their momentum careened them against the marble plinth, where Caravaggio's forehead took the brunt of the collision, knocking him out cold.

Alarms screamed. Lights flashed. Voices yelled. Vault-like doors began slamming down, closing off distant galleries. Thank God Em hadn't torn up his wings.

Groaning at the weight, every muscle in his back screaming, Matt managed to lift Caravaggio from the floor. Cradling the artist in his arms, Matt summoned all his strength and took two bold steps, opened his wings and bounded into the air.

The gawking, terrified guards stared as an angel in leather sideswiped the lights above the wide stairs, flew across the vaulted ceiling and vanished into French history paintings of 1650–1750.

Minutes after leaving Paris, Em emerged in a mist of melancholy and a cloud of green on to the floor of the Kelvingrove Art Gallery, in a clumsy fade from William Orchardson's *The Marriage of Convenience*. Moments later, wings gone, Matt faded out of the same painting, dragging Caravaggio behind him.

His shoulders ached. It didn't help that he'd had to fade through a Vermeer in London before the

Orchardson, each time with Caravaggio like a sack of coal on his back.

'Do you think he's concussed?' Em asked, staring at the unconscious figure on the gallery floor by their feet.

'Fine by me if he wakes up with a thumping good headache,' Matt said darkly.

'What are we going to do with him?'

Matt gazed at the artist, chewing his lip.

'You're thinking about letting him go again,' Em said. 'Aren't you? I'd love to hear that conversation. "I'm sure you won't mind, Vaughn, but we've disobeyed orders and let a rogue Animare go free because I fancied him."'

'I want to know what the Camarilla is,' said Matt.

'Caravaggio wasn't born in the age of the Internet, or he would never have given us the name,' said Em. 'Look it up.'

Matt ran a quick check on his phone. Nothing came up.

'The man's a loose cannon, Matt,' Em warned. 'We can't just let him go. He's lovely to look at, but totally unmanageable.'

Matt made a decision. 'Let's hide him for a while until we decide on a more permanent solution.'

'Vaughn has a permanent solution. Binding!'

'Caravaggio made it sound like this Camarilla were bad news. It would be nice to have a little advance warning on an enemy for a change,' said Matt stubbornly. 'He won't tell us who they are if we bind him, will he?'

Em sighed, but helped Matt to drag Caravaggio, sword clanking against the wooden floors, through the gallery to the nearest storage room. Matt shoved the artist inside, propping him against a mop and bucket. Locking the door behind them, they went in search of a better hiding place.

'We need somewhere nice,' Em said, scanning the walls.

'Now who's being soft?' Matt enquired. 'A jailer would be better.'

They headed into a gallery displaying many of the paintings of the Glasgow Boys. One painting was glowing, a pale blue light only an Animare or Guardian could detect.

'James Guthrie was an Animare,' said Em, staring at Guthrie's *A Funeral Service in the Highlands*. 'We could use that one.'

'I don't think a gathering of auld grieving Scotsmen would take kindly to an Italian rogue,' Matt observed. 'Although, it might be a laugh to imagine Caravaggio talking himself out of a thumping from a scowl of crofters. What about *Hard At It* instead? It's one of Zach's—'

Matt stopped.

'He's not dead,' Em said after a moment. 'You can talk about him, you know.'

In *Hard At It* the artist had set himself up on a windy Scottish beach, shielded from the elements by a white umbrella, and painted himself painting on a windy Scottish beach behind a white umbrella. During their studies at the Abbey, the twins had learned that many Animare had created paintings of themselves in paintings.

'*Hard At It* it is,' Em decided. 'Caravaggio will appreciate Guthrie's style. Plus he'll be safe from civilization – and himself. I remember reading that Guthrie carried a pistol among his painting supplies. He used it to shoot his dinner on his walk home.'

'And, behold, I am alive for evermore; and have the keys of hell and of death.'

*Revelation 1:18*

# FOURTH MOVEMENT

# 27

# A HIGHER CAUSE

With efficiency, sawhorses cordoned off the perimeter of the square. A crowd gathered behind the barricades, mobile phones pointed at the chaos surrounding the statue of Shakespeare, which had been tented. Some witnesses were staunching bloody noses, a handful wearing oxygen masks, and one or two were in the arms of paramedics, staggering towards ambulances.

The police commander pushed his way through a group of officers inside the tent.

'What the hell just happened here? Tell me this isn't all just for a punter stealing cigarettes.'

Patrol Officer Lakshmi Misra stood quietly to one side of the tent, watching her sergeant talking angrily on his mobile phone, waiting for her chance to duck out. Hired as part of a community policing initiative formed to advance minorities more quickly through the ranks, Lakshmi wasn't popular among the old guard, but she had talents and connections they couldn't begin to imagine. She was biding her time. She had big plans.

Lakshmi was the first female in her family to graduate from secondary school, never mind university and elite police training (a feat of obstinacy as much as hard work and intelligence). Lakshmi had always known what she wanted to do with her life. Year after year of doggedness, of working with her papa in the family's antique restoration business, of trying his patience with her questions, annoying him with what she'd learned at school or read in her many true-crime and mystery books, had eventually paid off with her papa's agreement to fund her education in criminology.

'Don't give me a reason to regret my decision to let you do this, Lakshmi,' her papa had said after the fast-tracked police training that had forced her to be in the best mental and physical shape of her life.

'I won't, Papa.'

He pulled her into a rare embrace.

'And never forget, my dear child, that our family serves a much higher cause than this,' he had whispered before releasing her into the embrace of her fellow recruits and the scowling handshake of her newly assigned division commander. 'Because one day you'll be called to take up arms for it.'

That higher cause was testing her loyalties more

quickly than she had anticipated. Here she was, slinking away from a crime scene and ducking behind a set of stairs to an emergency exit for the National Portrait Gallery, dialling a mobile number she had never dialled before. With a flash of doubt, she wondered if the number was even valid.

The phone rang a long time before the call was answered.

'Yes?'

'I've seen something,' whispered Lakshmi. 'I mean someone. He disappeared... Into a statue. It seemed to come alive right before—'

The voice on the other end was sharp. 'He animated in public?'

'He didn't draw – I mean, animate. He sang.'

There was a pause.

'Sang?' repeated the voice.

'Yes. It happened a few minutes ago. Behind the National Portrait Gallery... Hello? Hello?'

She'd been cut off.

*Ungrateful bastard. You could've at least said thanks.*

Back in the tent, her commander caught her eye with a scowl.

'I want units fanning out across London's theatre district, the Tube, the train stations,' he said. 'Suspect is a black male, approximately eighteen years of age, tall, lean build, shaved head, wearing a bluish-black jacket and dark jeans. Approach with caution, people. As you all know, we've been tracking these jewel thieves for weeks. He fits the profile. And if he is one of them, he could be dangerous.'

'Especially when singing,' Lakshmi muttered under her breath. 'I'll head back to the shop, sir, see if I can get any more information,' she said aloud.

'Didn't get enough last time round, Misra?' said her commander sarcastically. 'You may have got away with cutting corners on that high-speed training of yours, but we won't stand for it on the job.'

Lakshmi swallowed a retort and made her escape back towards the Strand. It was hard to stay positive sometimes.

At Old Worm's, she used the sleeve of her uniform to rub grime from the front window and peered inside. All she could discern were shadows. It looked like the clerks had got their precious key in the end. Not that she ever believed they didn't have it in the first place. Given how the young man had disappeared into the statue, this was no ordinary break-in, and the kid certainly wasn't a jewel thief as her commander believed. Insights she'd keep from any of her official reports.

She hit the number for the shop on her phone. Someone inside picked up the receiver and promptly set it down again. Lakshmi stared in through the window for a few more minutes, then banged on the door.

'Police,' she said through the letter box. 'I just want a word.'

Nothing.

Lakshmi was about to turn away when the lock turned and the door creaked open.

'What d'you want?'

It was the dishevelled clerk, the one with the cardigan and the bushy eyebrows.

'I'm sorry to trouble you again today, sir,' said Lakshmi, in her politest voice, 'but if you could give me a few more details on what happened in here this morning—'

'He was never inside this shop,' the clerk said, keeping his foot firmly against the bottom of the door to prevent Lakshmi from coming in. 'None of us were. And nothing has been stolen. We'd like the police to back off and leave us alone. Good day.'

He slammed the door, barely missing her feet and fingers. Her phone rang. It was the number she'd called earlier. Lakshmi jogged round the corner before answering. This time she told the person all that she knew.

'Whatever the kid was doing in the Little Shop of Horrors, it's sent the clerks into lock-down mode,' she said without preamble. 'Do you want me to stick around and see what happens next?'

'Let's shake them up a little. Try to gauge what's going on. Can you take the head clerk in for questioning? See what he has to say for himself under a little duress. Then let him go and watch him. Can you do that?'

'I think so,' said Lakshmi.

'I'm working on getting help to you, but we've got to bring that young man in before someone else does.'

# 28.

# MEMORIES OF YOU

Muffled traffic noise and the distant wail of sirens seeped down to Rémy through the cracks in the tiles of the old evacuation tunnel. He glanced at his watch, a knock-off Tag Heuer that Sotto had given him for his sixteenth birthday: 10.28 a.m. Only a few minutes since he'd fallen. Time to get out of here.

The statue was directly above him, which meant straight ahead should get him to the crypt beneath St Martin in the Fields. Part of the crypt had been turned into a café and a bookshop beneath the church, but he knew from the Professor there was a way round that.

Rémy walked south, stooping slightly to avoid brushing the tunnel roof, his eyes gradually adjusting to the eerie darkness. Every few minutes, the walls shook as Tube trains hurtled along nearby. The odours of human waste no longer fazed him; he'd been homeless for too many weeks. He ignored the rustling of rats scampering up ahead and away from him in the shallow murky water too. After several minutes, he reached an iron ladder up to a grate in the tiled ceiling. The grate looked as if it hadn't been used in a while. He tried it. Not surprisingly, it wouldn't budge.

Rémy began to feel anxious. What if the overhead world caved in on him? What if he died like a rat in these sewers, never able to finish his mother's quest? What if everything he'd done so far was for nothing?

He shimmied back down the ladder and paced up and down the tiny space, trying to bring his breathing under control. He knew that he'd have to return to Old Worm's and search the place more thoroughly. The painting may not have been in the cabinet, but that didn't mean it wasn't in the shop. The tablet, still thrumming faintly around his neck, had been loud and clear on that.

Rémy set his guitar case down and popped it open. Inside, he'd accumulated ten one-pound coins and assorted other change, plus five ceramic guitar picks from a fellow street busker, an ex-soldier suffering from PTSD. The soldier had been so impressed with Rémy's playing that he'd given him the picks. A photograph of his mother performing at the Royal Albert Hall with the Tulane University Ensemble lay among the change. At seventeen, Annie Dupree Rush had been the first black female to score a chair in the traditionally all-male group. Rémy sat back on his haunches against the wet tiles and stared at her, smiling behind her cello. His dad, a student from the London School of Economics, had been standing in the wings. After that concert Peter Rush decided he'd follow Annie Dupree's music anywhere in the world.

Rémy wiped his eyes with the back of his hand.

*Grow a pair, Rémy Dupree Rush!*

He gently replaced the photograph. Grabbing the guitar picks, he climbed back up the iron ladder and wedged a pick under the corroded lock. He pushed another as far into the other side of the latch as he could reach. Then he climbed back down and picked up his harmonica. He'd never conjured twice in such a short time. There'd be more ill effects, but they'd be better than suffocating beneath the streets of London.

Rémy let an image centre in his mind. He concentrated the way his mother had shown him, transforming the image into sound waves, letting the music rise in his imagination. He inhaled and exhaled, then put his harmonica to his lips and played a few bars from the Stones' 'You Can't Always Get What You Want'.

Seconds later, a loud concussive pop filled the chamber as the two picks expanded, blowing the lock off the rusted grate.

'But if you try,' grinned Rémy through his tears as he climbed.

# 29.

## MI CASA ES TU CASA

Rémy ached for sleep and silence as he approached the abandoned rail tunnel near South Kensington Station. The tunnel with its shantytown of boxes, tarps and crates had been his home for the past three weeks. He'd always had music playing in his head, telling him stories, riffing with the sounds in the world around him, but he'd never wished for silence before. It was different now.

*Please God, just for one night, peace and quiet.*

The Professor's tent stood under the tallest curve of the tunnel: a series of old blue construction tarps duct-taped together and held aloft with broom handles. It was furnished with an overstuffed armchair, an old-style primary-school desk, a cooler filled with whatever food and drink the Professor had managed to scavenge that day, a box of books and a bust of the philosopher Paracelsus. There was also a bicycle with a flat tyre and the Professor's camp bed, neatly made up with army surplus blankets and a thin pillow. Rémy's sleeping bag and backpack lay on the opposite side of the tent.

The Professor sat behind the primary-school desk, writing. In the short time Rémy had known him, the Professor was always writing; and yet when Rémy stole a look it wasn't writing like any he had ever seen, just lines and lines of repetitive numbers, patterns and glyphs. Rémy figured that, whatever the Professor was doing, it made perfect sense in his world.

'Success?' inquired the Professor without looking up.

'No,' said Rémy, setting his guitar case on the floor and flopping down in the armchair. He ran his hands across his shaved head, the growth prickling his palms.

'I'll need to go back and look more carefully some other time. I wish I knew what exactly I was looking for. I wish I'd known enough to help my mom with this search when she was alive. I wish—'

'My boy, don't punish yourself for what you could not have known. Those kinds of wishes are simply vanity disguised as regret. Now, tell me again what your mother told you.'

'"Find the Moor and find the painting",' Rémy repeated wearily. 'I've struck out with the painting and I've no idea what a Moor is, never mind where to find one.'

'Well, I may be able to help with the Moor.'

The Professor unfolded his large body from behind the tiny desk and pulled out a map, the kind that hung in libraries and classrooms. He picked up a broken umbrella and used it as a pointer.

Despite the exhaustion in his bones, Rémy knew better than to doze off. If he insulted his eccentric host, he was pretty sure he'd be asked to leave – and then where would he go? He unlaced his boots for comfort, but kept them on. Footwear was as precious as gold among the homeless. It could never leave your feet.

'In the Middle Ages through to the early fifteen hundreds,' the Professor began, 'many wealthy North African aristocrats migrated with their armies across the straits of Gibraltar, here and here.' He pointed to southern Spain with the handle. 'They established themselves in Granada and Cordoba in particular, building castles and palaces and many of the trade routes that eventually fuelled the economy in this part of the world.'

Rémy shifted his chair. 'So Moors are from North Africa?'

'Yes, by and large.'

'Were these Moors Muslim?'

'Many were. But Spain was a Catholic country. You have no doubt heard of the Spanish Inquisition?'

Rémy couldn't help himself. 'No one expects them, I can tell you that much.'

The Professor looked blank.

'I would question that position,' he said. 'The Inquisitors were well known and feared at the time. Various royal decrees issued between 1492 and 1501 ordered many of the Moors to convert or leave Spain forever. The Inquisition ensured that those who claimed to have converted, did so in the proper fashion.'

Rémy stifled a yawn. He was so damn tired.

'The Moors were known to be great philanthropists and supporters of the arts, especially music,' the Professor continued. 'One story in particular may be of interest to you. The story of a Moor and the most famous *castrato* of Renaissance Europe, Don Grigori de Cordoba.'

Rémy's drooping eyes flew open. *Castrato?*

'In the early part of the sixteenth century,' said the Professor. 'This *castrato* was celebrated in every theatre and court in Europe. For a long time, one of his main benefactors was a Moor known as the Caliph of Cadiz.'

The excitement that had flared in Rémy's heart died. This wasn't the Moor his mother had told him to find. He needed someone in the twenty-first century.

'Now,' the Professor continued, oblivious to Rémy's disappointment, 'it's a popular misconception that *castrati* have no testicles—'

'I wouldn't say popular,' muttered Rémy.

'—but it's not entirely true. To keep their pristine voices at a high-octave range, young boys had the endocrine ducts to their testicles sliced, so that their testicles would shrivel up. A eunuch had his testicles removed entirely, usually for quite different reasons.'

Rémy's empty stomach churned.

'It is widely believed that the Moor and the *castrato* duelled over money and went their separate ways. The *castrato* withdrew from the opera at the peak of his career and the height of his fame to accept a position as composer and personal musician at the court of Cardinal Rafael Oscuro, one of the most infamous Inquisitors of the period.'

Rémy loved listening to the Professor's stories, especially late at night when homesickness gripped his heart in a vice. But this lecture was pushing it after the day he'd had.

'I'm sorry, Professor,' he said, 'but what has any of this got to do with finding the Moor my mom told me to find? That guy must have died 500 years ago!'

The Professor's eyes were strangely dark. 'Time is much more wibbly wobbly than you think.'

'If it is, I'd like to wobble back at least a few months before any of this shit hit my fan.'

Rémy suddenly felt as if he had been plunged into a warm bath. His muscles, taut with fear and exhaustion, relaxed. His frustration fizzled. His headache faded, the sound from the pendant at his neck a distant thready hum. He looked at the Professor.

'How do you do that?'

'Do what?' asked the Professor, opening a carton of partially eaten KFC he had retrieved from a nearby dumpster.

Rémy stood in front of the Professor.

'My mom would calm me with her singing when I was little. I'd feel her lullabies in my head like a blanket wrapping my brain. You do the same thing, somehow.'

Rémy eyed his guitar and his backpack, in case he had to make a run for it.

'You made me trust you the moment I met you. I've seen you do it to others. You can calm a rowdy crowd and persuade them to fill your hat with cash. And not just because your stories are good.'

'What a curious thing to say,' murmured the Professor. 'Would you like a wing from this chicken in a box?'

Rémy ignored the offer. 'I've spent my entire life around magical secrets,' he said. 'There's something odd about you. If I should be worried, I'd like to know sooner rather than later.'

The Professor put the carton of chicken down and stared at the blue tarped wall of the tent.

'I am... different,' he said at last.

'No kidding,' said Rémy. It had been a hell of a journey from losing his mother in Chicago to a tent in London with a man who could control people with his mind. 'Are you even a real professor?'

'Perhaps not in the way you know. The one thing I have time for is reading. And libraries are the most hospitable environments for a person like me to pass my time. I have taken advantage of the best of the world's libraries over the years, trying to understand who I am and what my destiny may be.'

'And what have you discovered?'

The Professor switched his gaze back to Rémy. 'That I am meant to use my special talents to help you,' he said. 'It was kismet that you and I ran into each other that day.'

Rémy weighed the situation up. He was so far removed from his old life and any semblance of a normal future he'd once imagined for himself. What did he have to lose?

'OK. I'm happy to have your help,' Rémy said.

The Professor nodded briskly. 'We will make a start tomorrow.'

'Will you tell me more about the Moor I have to find?'

'I can do better than that. Tomorrow I will take you to see him.'

# 30.

# STILL FREAKY

Later that evening, Rémy returned to Old Worm's, waiting in the shadows at the end of the lane to be sure the shop was empty and the police were gone. The city was giving in to darkness, moonlight struggling to find its way between the buildings. Rémy was glad of the cover. He ducked round to the back of the shop, took out his penknife and jimmied the lock.

Someone had mopped the floor recently, the trail of the mop head still visible in places. Trying to ignore the increasing noise from the tablet around his neck, Rémy worked his way through the boxes and crates, emptying their contents on the floor, searching for canvases and paintings. He flicked through a selection of framed works stacked against one wall, many showing over-dressed young women playing harpsichords, men in austere outfits posing in front of mirrors or maps, and one or two landscapes with peasants chewing hay. Nothing resembled the painting he was tracking from his mother's journal. As a precaution, he slipped his harmonica from its sleeve and tucked it into his pocket. No harm being prepared should he run into trouble again.

The tablet hummed more loudly in his head as he moved in front of the antique cabinet once again. It was still empty. He sighed, scanning the papered walls and low-hanging animal heads nearby. It was like looking for a needle in a haystack after the haystack had been eaten by a herd of cows. The painting could be anywhere.

Rémy wanted to scream, to punch someone. He squeezed his fists until his nails stabbed into his palms. He leaned against the wall opposite the cabinet, biting the insides of his cheeks, tasting his sorrow.

*Jesus, Mom, why did you wait so long to tell me your secret? I could have shared the burden.*

The tablet was screaming now, burning hot against his skin. A floorboard creaked above him. The front door chimed. Someone was entering the shop. Yanking his hoodie over his head and turning the collar of his jacket up, Rémy slid soundlessly out of the rear door, back the way he had come. He jogged to the end of the lane in the growing dusk and headed across the Strand, dodging traffic and pedestrians. Keeping his head low to avoid CCTV cameras and eagle-eyed police, he failed to notice Lakshmi Misra following close behind him.

# 31.

# SCALDING TEA
# AND BURNING QUESTIONS

I f Hector Donet had to drink one more cup of weak, milky, police department tea without a side of chocolate digestive biscuits, he'd die. He was absolutely sure of it. Really die. His blood sugar was as low and his nerves were as frayed as a flag in a storm. That Indian copper had dragged him to the police station this afternoon to give an official report. Stupid bitch was digging, and digging too deeply was dangerous. He'd missed his lunch and his dinner because of her.

Hector had known the young man was a Conjuror as soon as he'd walked through the door. Perhaps if old Wendy hadn't screamed bloody murder at the sight of a black kid with a harmonica, panic might have been averted. She was becoming a liability in her old age, but her custom was valuable and her connections to be feared. At least she could be relied on not to show her face in a police station any time soon.

Given his regular caffeine and blood sugar fixes yesterday when he needed them most, Hector might have been willing to share an intriguing titbit or two with the police to keep them happy but throw them off the real trail. Instead, he had muttered, mumbled, huffed and puffed and stayed with the script. Yes, the shop's owner was an absentee landlord. He certainly had never met him. No, he didn't think the other staff had either. He was foreign, from the Costa Brava or Majorca or somewhere like that. Topless beaches there, and all that sort of European stuff. Would you want to hang around an old shop in London if you had all that Spanish sun? Might he have a cuppa? Black, please. There were three clerks and two security guards who helped with transporting their imports and exports. Yes, he was quite sure none of them had actually ever met the proprietor. Thanks, love, that'll hit the spot. Nice and hot. Yes, of course, he got paid. Would you bloody well work for nothing? In British Pound Sterling, thank you very much. None of that European Monopoly money. He would accept nothing else. His cheque was deposited regular as clockwork into his building society account. No, he had no idea from what bank in Spain. That was the whole point of direct deposit, wasn't it, you never had to set foot in a bank? Bloody thieves, all of them, anyway. No. Never seen the young ruffian before. Why was he not in school or working? What's the world coming to, when a busker can bring out the police in such force, but when someone steals a pint of milk from his front steps there's never one in the neighbourhood? Damn jewel thieves have everyone's knickers in a twist, looking twice at anything unusual in the area. Whoops, clumsy me, spilling scalding hot tea on you lass. That will blister something rotten.

He could still hear the yelp of pain from the girl he'd burned with the tea as he strode down the street towards the shop, checking to see if anyone was following. He was still concerned about the Indian copper – sharp as a tack, that one.

It was too bad Don Grigori had not been able to neutralize the boy in Chicago as planned. Instead, he'd had to return to the painting to recover from his injuries. And now it appeared the boy had somehow tracked Don Grigori back here. What a cock-up!

Hector scanned the street one more time as he approached the shop, keys in hand. No sign of Miss Nosy Parker. Just the usual evening crowds on their way to the theatres and clubs.

Locking the front door behind him, he headed towards the back of the shop. Then he stopped dead at the sight of a man grinning down at him from the balcony.

'How did you get in here?'

'You forgot to secure your fire escape. Naughty naughty.' Lafferty adjusted his navy pea coat and fiddled with a penny whistle from South Africa worth about fifty pounds.

'Don't touch the merchandise, Lafferty, for—' Hector

snatched the penny whistle from Lafferty's big hands, cleaned the reed inside the whistle with a soft brush and wiped the outside with a dry cloth. He set it under the counter where he had left it.

'Can you still hear that terrible noise in your head?' asked Lafferty suddenly. 'I've had a headache all day.'

'That'll be the Taser, you fool,' said Hector.

'He caught me on my blind side,' said Lafferty defensively. 'Otherwise, no way he'd have sat me down like that.' Bereft of the penny whistle, he started fiddling with his Taser instead, safely looped back on his belt. 'How'd he find this place anyway? It's not like you can type directions into your satnav.'

Hector was tired of Lafferty already. Brawn he may have had in abundance, but brain was lacking. He wished the man would leave. He had travel arrangements to make and a boy to find.

'We've underestimated him,' he said. 'A mistake for which I will throw myself at the mercy of the Grand Inquisitor, when I am finally able to bow down before his everlasting light.'

Lafferty looked blank. Unsurprising. The man was an idiot, Hector thought. He had no idea of the importance of what they were protecting in this place. He just counted the cash.

'We have to find the boy,' Hector said fretfully. 'We need to be sure everything is ready. We cannot fail now we are so close.'

Lafferty raised his fingers to his forehead in a mock salute.

Hector slammed his hands on the counter, rattling the cash register.

'You are a foot soldier in this army and you insult your superiors. The Camarilla have been protecting the Grand Inquisitor for centuries, and I have not risen through their ranks over the years to be taken down by the likes of you! You will not defile this sacred space with your slack-jawed behaviour. If you had captured the stupid boy this morning, we would not have to alter plans that have been eternities in the making!'

Lafferty got up and walked over to the old cabinet with the brass hinges, pulling open its doors and running his fingers absently along its fretwork of drawers. 'Here's what I'd really like to know, Mister Doughnut.'

'It's Doe-net, you twit,' said Hector furiously. 'My family were bankers to Spanish royalty. We've financed more countries and crowns than you've had hot dinners.'

'But you're Scottish,' said Lafferty.

'My family goes all the way back to Queen Juana of Spain herself.'

'Never heard of her. My family goes back to good old Alfred.'

'Queen Juana was a woman of great learning,' Hector hissed, beyond furious now. 'Without her particular kind of magic, our Grand Inquisitor would never have survived.'

'Whatever, Mr Doughnut,' said Lafferty, turning to check out the antique cabinet backed against the far wall. 'As I was saying, here's what I'd really like to know—'

Behind him, Lafferty heard a soft whistling sound like a breeze through bulrushes. The sound wrapped itself around him.

'Don't you worry your tiny brain with questions,' said a soft, high-pitched voice. 'We pay you to do your job, not to think.'

Lafferty was about to comment on his boss's sudden dialect change when a bluebottle the size of his thumb crawled up the side of the cabinet to flutter in front of his face. Another crawled out of the cabinet lining. When he lifted his hand to swat it away, Lafferty realized his entire hand was a glove of hungry black flies, and they were shredding his skin.

# 32.

# DEATH AND DUST

The flies stuck fast to Lafferty's skin. He ran screaming across the shop, waving his hands hopelessly in the air. Bits of his skin started falling in strips on to the wooden planks of the shop's floor. Lafferty flapped and flailed for a few more minutes, but a cluster of the flies had found a tasty vein on his wrist. Within minutes he was dead in a pool of his own blood, a grin of terror frozen on his face.

'He was a liability,' said Don Grigori, slipping a pitch pipe into the inside pocket of a black bespoke suit. 'And, worse, a terrible bore. You simply can't find good men these days.' He adjusted his cuffs. 'I must admit I do quite like the fashions of this time, Hector. This English tailor knows his craft. Make sure you reward him well. We may need him again soon, when His Eminence is back among us.'

Hector bowed, ignoring the flies buzzing round Don

Grigori's head. 'It's an honour for his family to have been of service to the Camarilla.'

Kneeling, Don Grigori scooped a handful of buzzing bluebottles from what remained of Lafferty's raw pink flesh and white cartilage. Cupping them in his hands, he puffed air at their wings, watching them flutter on his palm before brushing them back on to the body.

'Should I clean that up?' Hector asked.

Don Grigori ran his slender fingers over an animal skin, sending dust motes dancing into a ribbon of sunlight piercing the filthy latticed windows. Then he sat on a carved mahogany chair and crossed his legs, his elegant hands smoothing the already perfect crease on his trousers. Even after only one day outside the painting, Hector noticed Don Grigori's recently repaired skin was thinning, his complexion becoming translucent and jaundiced.

'Leave my children to their work,' he said. 'Tell me what you have learned about the boy's whereabouts.'

'According to my sources,' Hector said, 'he conjured his disappearance and vanished beneath a statue of Shakespeare.'

Don Grigori smiled. 'Ah, Shakespeare.'

Hector continued. 'The police believe the boy is part of the gang of jewel thieves who've been plaguing this part of the city in recent months. The sooner we can relieve them of this notion, the better for us.'

'How so?'

'When the heat from the police cools, the boy will be more open in his movements, making it easier for our network of spies to catch sight of him.'

'It is an affront that the boy has escaped again,' Don Grigori said irritably. 'I must share the blame for our failure to stop him in Chicago. I'd never encountered two conjurors at the same time, especially a mother and a son. I was unprepared for their powerful bond. It will not happen again.'

'The boy's mother had been trouble for a long time,' said Hector, flicking a fly from his forehead. 'Taunting us with her music at the Albert Hall, no less.'

'Indeed,' said Don Grigori. 'And now her son comes charging into our plans with his lance tilted.'

'Should we delay the journey?' asked Hector. 'We could stay here a little longer.'

Don Grigori cupped Hector's chin and tipped his face upwards. His gaze was ice blue. Hector shivered.

'We will leave tomorrow as planned. The boy has worked faster than I could have imagined after his mother's death. He has her journal to guide him, of course. When he is ours, we must destroy it. For a weak woman, she somehow managed to uncover our plans.'

'The boy will be ours soon enough,' said Hector.

Don Grigori nodded. 'And when he is, our journey to the Second Kingdom can proceed. Until then, prepare your... what is your word?'

'Our network, signor?'

'This age lacks poetry, Hector.' Don Grigori sighed. 'Use your network, then, and search this city for the boy. When you find him, bring him to me.'

'I know someone in a unique position to help us,' said Hector. 'Until now, this person has been a rather reluctant member of our cabal. Perhaps it is time to call in our favours.'

A bluebottle landed on Don Grigori's polished brogues. He leaned forward and let it flutter to the back of his hand, where it folded its wings against its bulbous body. The *castrato* pinched the fly between his fingers and dropped it into his mouth.

'I trust I can leave this matter with you, Hector,' Don Grigori said, floating up off the chair. 'Don't let me down again.'

Hector bowed and tried not to think about Lafferty's corpse.

# 33.

# MAGIC AND REVELATION

The inside of the church was cold; Matt and Em's breath fogged the air. Em stomped up and down, trying to drive some life to her toes. They had deposited Caravaggio on the beach with Guthrie, surprisingly without much fuss from either man, and grabbed a late meal before returning to HQ. Now it was just a question of keeping warm. Em was in leggings, boots, fingerless gloves and an Argyle sweater Jeannie had knitted for her birthday. She layered this over a T-shirt, plus an oversized cardigan she'd found in a closet in the living quarters upstairs. Matt's hair was loose on his shoulders and damp from the sea air. He was dressed in a vintage Bob Dylan T-shirt, skinny black jeans, boots and a tartan blanket he'd rustled from Vaughn's bedroom. His shades were on the top of his head, his eyes on full-tilt freaky.

'I've a new assignment for you,' said Vaughn, turning the screen of his laptop to face the twins. 'According to a source, there was an incident at a shop just off the Strand involving this young man.'

Vaughn showed them a photo that looked like it had come from someone's phone. The twins didn't ask how his source had taken such a clear picture given that their own source was unconscious in a nineteenth-century Scottish landscape. The twins looked closely at the image.

'The clerks in the store are being uncooperative, claiming the lad was never there, despite the fact that the police have footage of him running across the rooftops nearby.'

'Did he steal something? People shoplift all the time,' said Matt, looking at the photograph. 'Why did they go all super SWAT on him?'

'It's wrong, but his colour probably made him an easy target,' said Em with disgust.

'I think it may have something to do with the jewel thieves who've been upsetting wealthy shoppers in the city centre,' said Vaughn.

'Still don't get why this is Orion's concern,' said Matt.

'Right after this incident, a phone call came in to our London headquarters from one of our sources in the field. My source said that the young man evaded capture by disappearing into a statue of Shakespeare in an explosion of light.'

'That sounds like an Animare,' said Em, clutching her mug of tea for warmth. Her gloves weren't helping.

'That's what HQ thought at first,' said Vaughn. 'But he didn't draw his way in. He altered reality with music.

Specifically, with his voice. Which means he's not an Animare, he's a *Conjuror*.'

Em put her cup down and Matt shifted his chair forward as Vaughn opened a new screen, typed in a password and clicked through to the pages of an illuminated manuscript on Orion's database of grimoires and other ancient documents.

'This is a facsimile of Agrippa's *Compendium of Magic*,' he told the twins. 'It's one of only two manuscripts we've ever discovered that mention Conjurors, and trust me we have looked. We had assumed the supernatural line of Conjurors had died out during the African Diaspora, when the Atlantic slave trade seized and scattered African peoples.'

'Conjurors are African?' asked Matt.

'What little we know suggests their origins are somewhere in the Middle East or the African continent,' said Vaughn, 'but we don't have enough evidence to know more than that. Occasionally, one of Orion's researchers will come across an image or reference, but that's not happened in decades. I don't think anyone's even looking for them any more.'

Em leaned closer to read the Latin text beneath the image of an angelic-looking African youth playing a golden lyre.

'"A Conjuror alone can lure demons to the underworld with his music,"' she translated aloud.

Matt, who was not as fluent in Latin as Em, pointed

at an illuminated quotation set off with whirls of what was likely gold leaf. 'What does this one say?'

Em ran possible phrasing through her head. '"Only when the chord is true and the voice is clear will the Second Kingdom fall",' she said. 'There's a faded bit here too, with a few words missing, which says something about, "when the Camarilla rise, the fallen will walk the earth".'

*I've heard that word before, Matt. Camarilla.*

*Me too. Don't say anything else in my head, Em. Vaughn's too good.*

'What are you two buzzing back and forth about?' said Vaughn, eyeing them.

'Only that these phrases sound like an ancient apocalyptic prophecy,' said Matt quickly. 'And you know the problem with apocalyptic prophecies? For people like us, they're a royal pain in the arse.'

Em grinned. *Good save.*

Vaughn burst out laughing.

'You're right,' he said. 'But if this young man really is a Conjuror, then he's a rarity, and we have to bring him in for his own protection. I need you both to fade to London and take a closer look at the statue where he disappeared. If he is a Conjuror, the Council of Guardians must be informed immediately. Then someone with more experience in the field will be assigned to bring him in.'

Em and Matt both opened their mouths at the same time. Vaughn held up a warning hand.

'If you want to be part of my Orion team, you need to learn to play with others. Don't get too close to him or anyone else connected with the police investigation. Just investigate the scene and then report back. Understood?'

*I'm thinking this is probably not a good time to tell him about Caravaggio.*

*You think?*

'Understood,' the twins said in unison.

Vaughn clicked over to another screen on his computer. A map of the centre of London came up.

'The statue is directly behind the National Gallery and the shop is in a quiet lane off the Strand. You can fade from our Vermeer here to another one in the National Gallery. Go to the shop. See if you can find out why its staff are not cooperating with the police. My gut tells me they know more than they're saying.'

He pulled an accordion folder from a locked cabinet, tucked in an alcove below the Turner, in the north transept.

'Can we inspirit them into cooperating?' Em asked.

'Use your powers sparingly,' Vaughn advised, sifting through the folder's contents. 'As far as the Council is concerned, you're probationary Orion agents only, which means you're not supposed to take on cases without my close supervision. Do not let me down.'

He handed Em and Matt each an old-fashioned flip phone, an ID card, a credit card from the Bank of Scotland and a hundred pounds in cash.

'This is ancient,' said Matt, examining the phone.

'It's better than it looks. It has a direct line to Orion's switchboard,' Vaughn said. 'And it takes decent pictures and video. Don't use your iPhones for Orion business, they are too easily traced.'

Em picked up the ID card and read aloud, '"Orion Insurance Inc." We're insurance agents?'

'Of course you are,' said Vaughn. 'We insure that Animare and their Guardians are protected from those who will do them harm.'

'Wait a minute. You said that Orion has knowledge of only two ancient manuscripts mentioning Conjurors,' said Matt. 'If Agrippa's *Compendium of Magic* is one of them, what's the other?'

Vaughn rubbed his hand over his stubbled chin. 'The other text with a reference is the Apocalypse of John.'

Em froze. 'You've got to be kidding,' she said.

'What?' said Matt.

'The Apocalypse of John,' said Em, shivering despite all her layers, 'is the original version of the bible's Book of Revelation.'

## 34.

# THE PRICE OF FREEDOM

'Matt, wake up!'

Matt rolled over on the leather couch tucked in an alcove of the Orion chapel, pulling the tartan blanket over his head. Em tugged the blanket back, and the static stood Matt's hair up in crazy curls.

'We have to let Caravaggio go,' said Em.

Matt yawned, pulling his hair off his face and twisting it into a loose knot. His eyes shifted from blue with gold flecks to green with silver, then settled to a blazing cobalt. 'Why are we talking about this in the middle of the night? You're the one who said he ought to be bound.'

'Hear me out,' said Em. 'Caravaggio said he had information he'd be willing to trade with us in return for his freedom.'

Matt frowned, still bleary with sleep. 'OK, but unless his information threatens the continued existence of the universe, I don't see why I can't sleep another couple of hours first.'

'Because,' said Em, 'Caravaggio is the one who mentioned the Camarilla to us first. That's why I knew the word. "The Camarilla is back", remember? We've got to find out what he knows.'

For a second Matt didn't move. Then he tugged on his jeans and grey T-shirt while he hopped on the cold stone floor. 'Next time, Em, open with that.'

When they were dressed and Matt had found his shades, they faded from the Turner into a Dutch painting called *Interior of an Imaginary Gothic Church*, where they caught their breath behind a Gothic column.

'So nice to have young Animare visit us again,' said a young woman in the painting as Matt and Em prepared to fade on into the Kelvingrove Art Gallery, where the Dutch painting hung. 'Don't leave it so long next time.'

'We'll be back soon, and I'm sure you'll be as beautiful as ever,' said Matt, bowing gallantly.

The young woman tittered as the twins fell from the painting in a rush of ochre and pink light, landing on the gallery floor.

The twins wasted no time fading into Guthrie's *Hard At It*, where they'd abandoned Caravaggio the day before. They jogged past the artist with a nod and tromped along the beach, sand filling their boots, until they spotted Caravaggio spread out on his back behind a grassy dune, a flagon of ale in one hand, the other tucked behind his head.

'You'd better not let Guthrie see that booze,' said Matt, sitting down next to Caravaggio. 'He can be an angry teetotaller.'

Caravaggio offered Matt and then Em a swig.

'Bit early for us,' answered Em, noticing the etchings on the rocks next to the artist of four flagons of ale and what looked like a couple of turkey legs and a loaf of bread.

'As you like, my friends,' said Caravaggio. 'But since I've no wretched idea whether it's morning, noon or night, I am at the mercy of my appetites.' He sat up and drank heartily from the jug. 'Are you planning on keeping me here much longer?'

'That depends,' said Em.

'On what?'

'On what you tell us about the Camarilla,' said Matt, lifting his shades.

Caravaggio started. 'Good God, your eyes!' he said in wonder. 'What colours! I've never seen anything like them.'

Matt's stomach flipped as Caravaggio cupped his chin to get a better look.

'We need the information,' Matt said, making no attempt to break loose, 'and we need your word you'll help us if we need you to. Then we'll let you go.'

Caravaggio continued to stare deeply into Matt's eyes. Neither man moved. Em waved her hand between them.

'Hellooo!' she said drily. 'I hate to break up this lust fest, but we need to know what information you think is worth your freedom.'

Caravaggio reluctantly let go of Matt's face. Matt, equally reluctant, sat back. The artist took another long swig of ale and addressed both of them.

'Give me your word as sworn agents of Orion that you will grant me my freedom in return for information that, in your ridiculously undisciplined modern vernacular, will blow your socks off.'

'Here's what we'll do,' said Em. 'You tell us what you've learned, and we'll check it out. If it turns out to be relevant, then we'll free you from Guthrie's watch and let you wander in the world for one month before we come after you again.'

'Shall we shake on it?' Caravaggio asked.

'Just blow our socks off,' said Matt.

'Any time, my friend,' said Caravaggio, gripping Matt's hand.

Em fake-gagged. Matt shook his head. Caravaggio stretched out on the sand, grinning.

'The first I heard of the Camarilla was during the time of the Spanish Inquisition,' he began. 'Some of the members of this cabal were Animare and Guardians like us. Others were alchemists and sorcerers, men and women dedicated to the study of dark magic. They were mostly based in Spain and Italy. When the Camarilla fell out of favour with the Spanish throne, many people thought they went underground, out of sight, ready to return when they were needed again. Others thought they sailed to the New World and established themselves there. Whatever happened, there's been no sign of them until this century. And now it seems they're operating again.'

'You said people thought they would return when they were needed,' said Em. 'Needed for what?'

'They were said to be protecting a supernatural being, a demon or monster of some kind. Their mission was to hunt and destroy those who could destroy him,' said Caravaggio, sipping from his flagon. 'They had their tentacles in lots of endeavours – the trades, the arts, even the Church.

'They sound like a kind of supernatural mafia,' said Em.

'I know of your mafiosi,' said Caravaggio, wiping his mouth with his sleeve. 'The Camarilla are far more dangerous.' He leaned over and brushed a curl from Matt's forehead. 'Your eyes are quite bewitching.'

Em glared.

'Enough,' said Matt, slipping his shades back on. 'We're on the clock.'

Caravaggio grinned, and continued. 'Not long ago, I found myself enjoying the generous hospitality of a Brueghel wedding. While I was appreciating the talents of one of the stable boys, I overheard a conversation between two Animare whom I recognized as Camarilla.'

'How did you know they were Camarilla?' asked Em.

'Members of the Camarilla wear a brand,' said Caravaggio. 'I recognized the mark on the wrist of one of the men.' He grabbed a stick and quickly sketched on the sand, three straight lines with one curved line crossing at either end of the three. 'It looked like this.'

'It looks like a harp,' said Em.

'Did you see where the men went?' asked Matt.

'I'm afraid I was quite distracted when they faded out of the painting,' said Caravaggio. 'The stable boy really was most adept.'

'Matt, we have to go,' said Em, standing and brushing sand from her jeans. 'Vaughn expects us to be in London in an hour.'

'Am I free to leave?' Caravaggio asked hopefully.

'Not just yet,' said Matt. 'We could have discovered a lot of that information from our own archives. What else do you have for us?'

'I have nothing else.'

'Well, enjoy the Scottish sunshine,' said Matt, getting up.

'Wait!' Caravaggio said, catching Matt's arm. 'On my wanderings in and out of my favourite works of art, I may have noticed that someone is stealing musical instruments from paintings.'

# 35.

## TIME TO GO

'You two are up early,' said Vaughn, pouring himself a cup of coffee and sitting next to Em at the small kitchen table upstairs in the church's living quarters.

'Anxious to get on our way to London, I guess,' said Em, sipping the tea she'd hastily made as soon as they'd returned from the Guthrie painting.

Her tall boots stood beside her chair. Vaughn's eyes narrowed as he leaned over and tipped one of the boots upside down. 'Sand?'

Em grabbed the boots and quickly tugged them on.

'Do you remember when I was younger and my dreams sometimes animated into reality when I was nervous or scared?'

Vaughn relaxed. 'I remember. Jeannie was always destroying handsome vampires or flying wizards with her frying pan at breakfast. So what was this one about?'

Em projected embarrassment as strongly as she could. 'Do you really want to know?'

'Nope,' said Vaughn, following the twins downstairs and into the church. 'I do not. Now, don't forget these.' He handed two new sketchpads from his desk drawer as the twins prepared to fade through the Vermeer to London. 'Use discreetly.'

Em shoved her sketchpad into her Emily the Strange messenger bag she wore slung over one shoulder. Suddenly guilt and longing pinged through her, and her stomach twisted. The bag had been a Christmas present from Zach.

'Ready?' asked Matt, opening his pad, charcoal in hand. Em could feel his excitement wash over her, chasing away the crazy butterflies in her gut.

'Check the statue for any residual evidence of animation,' Vaughn told them as Matt sketched. 'Then interview the clerks in the shop. If you get any leads on our Conjuror, that would be great too. But no more than that, OK?'

Matt was already outlining the main elements in the Vermeer, using the side of his hand to smudge and create texture.

'Oh,' Vaughn added, 'and if you need a direct line to Orion, use the phones I've given you. The operator will tell you where your nearest possible fade might be, in case you get lost or stuck.'

Em gripped her brother's shoulder as he drew, his hand flying over the page, lines of light shooting from his fingertips, coiling chimneys of mist building around them. Em's feet broke into particles of light and ribbons of shimmering colour. She felt her body tilt, and her limbs became weightless. In a burst of brilliant blue, she and Matt faded into *Girl Interrupted at Her Music Lesson*.

# 36.

## MAKING THE HEADLINES

Penelope Flanagan was rolling up the steel shutters protecting her granddad's newsagent's on Exhibition Road. The shop was a quick walk from the Victoria and Albert Museum, one of the world's foremost centres of excellence for the decorative arts: a fact not lost on Penelope, who wanted to become a fashion designer.

Even though it meant getting up early, Penelope didn't mind being the first one at the shop during her summer holidays. Most of her pleasure at opening the shop alone was her ritual with the newspapers. Penelope loved the feel, the smell, and the touch of them. She loved cutting the strings that bound the stacks waiting for her at the kerb, and being the first to smell the ink and scan the screaming headlines. Penelope was a news junkie like her granddad and, although her technology kept her connected to the world every second of every day, she appreciated the ritual and its connection to the Victorian newsies who had once flooded the street, as well as the bond it gave her to her granddad, who still marked the times of his life by the headlines that stood outside his shop door.

Penelope carried the tabloids inside first. She was about to return to the kerb for *The Times* and the *Telegraph* when the face on one of the papers struck her as familiar. She cut the strings, put aside the broadsheet ad for the sandwich board, and took a closer look.

It was a picture of a young black man, about the same age as her, looking lost amid a crowd of white tourists. Penelope read the caption: 'Have you seen this man?'

According to the story, the unidentified teenager had evaded a wide net cast by the London police yesterday after a suspected robbery at a shop off the Strand.

It was definitely him. Penelope had no doubt about it. She'd seen him that morning, lurking behind the café next door. His jacket, an expensive Belstaff, and his good looks had caught her eye. What was a young homeless person doing with such an expensive jacket?

She put on the kettle and thought about whether she wanted the bother of calling the police and being dragged into the drama of it all.

# 37.

## TRIFLING DETAILS

'How long do we have to wait?' asked Rémy, shoving his hands deep into his jacket pockets. He'd switched his hoodie for a long-sleeved T-shirt after seeing his picture splashed across the morning papers while scavenging for breakfast.

'Impatience is one of your more serious character flaws, my friend,' said the Professor. 'If you are not careful, it will be your downfall.'

Rémy scanned the man standing in front of him. The Professor was dressed in a navy wool pullover, a yellow scarf, a tweed jacket with suede patches on the elbows, green corduroys, black socks and sandals. Every item had belonged to at least two or three other men before him and sported their own distinctive odours. His thick belt studded with silver that looked like it belonged to a pirate, was fastened around the outside of his jacket.

'While you, of course, have no flaws at all, Professor,' Rémy observed.

'My flaws are neither here nor there,' the Professor replied, pulling a baseball cap down over his eyes. 'You are the issue at hand… Aha.'

A nondescript white delivery van was pulling up at the loading dock of the Victoria and Albert Museum.

'If you hurry,' said the Professor, 'you can help them carry the trays of packaged food inside for the vending machines. They will not challenge your presence as a service worker. The crew is always changing.'

Rémy checked the street. There were a couple of people on their phones marching to the Tube. An elderly man was smoking a cigarette and checking out the menu in a restaurant window, while his dog dumped on the establishment's stoop. The traffic was sparse, but it was not yet six.

Rémy had come to notice that when you were homeless, time moved outside any understandable social rhythm. The constructs that shaped how time passed for most people didn't exist when you lived on the street. The only reason Rémy knew the time this morning was that he'd noted it on the clock above the flower-market entrance when they'd crawled out of the sewer tunnel.

'Stay hidden until the museum opens to the public,' the Professor reminded him. 'You will be less conspicuous. Hide in a ladies' bathroom. Most of the cleaning staff are women, and they will have cleaned those stalls already.'

'How do you know that?'

The Professor adjusted his scarf. 'I've been around for long enough to know the answers to many of life's conundrums. Go!' he added with a gentle push. 'They are already unloading the trifles. I have somewhere else to be.'

Rémy cut quickly between two double-decker buses and into the delivery bay. As smooth as silk, he lifted a white plastic tray of yoghurt shakes from the back of the lorry, and caught up with two of the delivery workers as they pushed through the flapping rubber doors to the dock.

# 38.

# CASTING CALL

The twins studied Shakespeare carefully. The entire base of the statue was rippling in waves of pale blue light. Even after a full twenty-four hours, Shakespeare had not yet recovered from the Conjuror's powerful animation. Strips of yellow police tape fluttered from the arms of the statue in the cool breeze, while two uniformed officers stood nearby.

'How are your eyes?' asked Em.

'Fine.'

Em brushed flecks of blue paint from the arm of her over-sized sweater. 'Do you think the Conjuror left any prints on the statue?'

'I doubt it,' answered Matt, scanning the shops and the doorways surrounding the square. The morning sunlight was creating frissons of colour in his peripheral vision. 'Unless one of the crime-scene crew is an Animare too, they won't notice anything unusual.'

'Maybe you can use your 'gator eyes to see what actually happened.'

'Don't call them that.'

'That's what they're like,' Em persisted. 'A third eyelid drops over your eyes and pow! You see the past.'

'You're a laugh riot.'

'So can you?'

Since the incident at the Kirk, Matt had been practising, learning to control the way his eyes behaved in places where the past hung heavily in the air. He concentrated on the statue, but with no results. He wondered if his eyes had trouble with anything too recent.

'Nothing,' he said reluctantly. 'Wait... Over there.' He pointed across the square. 'Near that rubbish bin. Just outside the barricade. See?'

Em followed Matt's finger, but couldn't see anything out of the ordinary.

'Start at Shakespeare and then follow the trail of light,' Matt said. 'It begins outside that café.'

'I see it now. Wait here,' said Em. She jogged over to the café, where Matt saw her stop at the litter bin. With a quick glance over her shoulder, she scooped something from the bin and pocketed it.

*What have you got?*

*Walk, Mattie. I'll show you when no one's watching.*

Matt followed Em out of Leicester Square. They cut across St Martin's Lane, and in a few minutes were in a quiet alley off the Strand, only a few short steps from their next stop in London.

'Show me,' Matt ordered, holding out his hand.

Em dropped the iPod into his palm triumphantly. 'It had light all over it,' she said. 'I'm guessing our Conjuror dropped it.'

Matt studied the iPod. It was an old model. Attaching his own ear buds, he pressed play. Almost at once, Em saw him rear backwards, tearing the buds from his ears.

'Man, that's nasty,' he said. 'White noise, the kind you get when the TV isn't working properly.'

'Weird,' said Em, putting one ear bud in her ear. 'Who listens to white noise?'

'Forget the iPod for now,' said Matt, pointing towards a doorway. 'We have bigger problems. Look.'

A sign on the door of Old Worm's Curiosities and Ancient Alchemies read, 'Closed Until Further Notice.'

'Can you hear that?' said Em, listening. 'It's like a buzzing.'

'Maybe there's a wasps' nest in the rafters,' Matt suggested.

They both looked up at the thick wooden beams running above the shop's latticed windows.

'I think it's coming from inside,' said Em. She jiggled the shop's door handle, then slipped her sketchbook out of her bag.

'Hold up there, Quick Draw,' said Matt. 'Let's

animate somewhere not quite as visible. Round the back.'

As they slipped into the narrow alley next to the shop, a huge bluebottle bombed Matt, getting caught in his hair.

'Ow!' he yelped, ducking. 'What the— that bluebottle bit me!'

'Bluebottles don't bite, you idiot. Come on.'

The flies were worse near the heavy old door at the back of the shop. They were the size of stag beetles, buzzing in and out through the keyhole and underneath the door where the stoop was uneven.

'Have you ever seen—' Em began.

Matt tapped his temple. Em reframed the question inside her mind.

*Have you ever seen black flies this big? It's like they're on steroids.*

*Never. Definitely something weird going on here.*

They both heard a door open and close into the tiny courtyard of the office next door. A spiral of smoke rose over the wall, together with the sound of someone flipping through a magazine.

'Hey,' Matt said, popping his head up over the wall.

There was a scream and the sound of a dropped magazine. 'Jesus! I nearly had a stroke. Who are you?'

'Didn't mean to scare you. Can I have a word?'

A gate opened in the wall and a young woman peered out. 'How can I help?'

Matt offered her his most disarming smile. 'Matt Calder, Orion Insurance.'

*Could you have sounded any more like James Bond?*

'We're not buying,' said the woman. 'Sorry.'

'I'm not here to sell you anything,' Matt reassured her. 'I just have a couple of questions about what happened yesterday at the shop next door.'

The woman relaxed. 'Checking to see if it was an inside job? I'm Jen Kolasa, by the way. Jennifer. My dad owns this place. Kolasa Casting Agency, that's us.'

Em rolled her eyes. Jen fancied Matt.

'Can't imagine who'd steal anything from that ghoulish place,' Jen went on. 'It attracts a weird clientele and, let me tell you, that's saying something coming from me: I work with actors. I once saw them carrying a coffin inside. I'm pretty sure they're all Satan worshippers. The manager's a nut-job for sure.'

'So what happened yesterday?' asked Matt.

'I saw him,' Jen said. 'The guy everyone's saying is a jewel thief. He jumped from our roof on to that one over there and then he disappeared down the lane towards St Martin's.'

'What did he look like?'

'His picture was in the paper this morning, didn't you see? Black. Tall. Kinda looked like a young Lenny Kravitz. Even had a guitar case on his back.'

'Jennifer?' came a shout from inside the office. 'How long does a fag break take? The phone's ringing off the hook in here! If I have to take one more call about the audition times for Disney's *Twelve Knights*, I won't be responsible for my actions!'

'That's my da,' said Jen. She seemed reluctant to end the conversation. 'I ought to go.'

'One more question,' said Matt. 'Was the shop open when the break-in happened?'

'I know they're saying no one was in,' said Jen, 'but it was definitely open. Right before I saw the black guy jump across the roof, I heard someone inside playing the harmonica. They were really good, and I remember looking out of the window to see if someone was cadging for money. We try to discourage that. Street's too narrow, and we get famous people coming in here a lot to make audition tapes. It's bad for business.'

'Jennifer! Get your bloody arse back to your desk now!'

'I'm coming, Da!' Jen shouted. She pulled an apologetic face at Matt, then fluttered her eyelashes. 'Sorry. Feel free to come by and interrogate me again any time.'

She slammed the gate behind her.

'Thank God for you, Sherlock,' said Em. 'I was as good as invisible.'

'Why thank you, Ms Watson,' Matt said with a wink. 'If the shop was open, that means the police report about not getting into the building because the owner was out of the country was bullshit. They lied to the police, or the police lied on the report.' He glanced at

Old Worm's ancient back door again. 'Were there that many flies before?'

'Oh my God, no,' said Em, staring at the mound of fat flies on the stoop. She looked a little sick. 'What happened?'

'We need to get inside that shop,' said Matt, pulling out his sketchpad.

Em sighed. 'I was afraid you were going to say that.'

# 39.

# OPEN FOR VISITORS

Finding a toilet stall he could hide in was more difficult than Rémy thought it would be. Eventually, he found a staff bathroom on the lower level of the museum and broke the lock. Once inside, he sat up on the cistern, his feet on the seat and his guitar case balanced between his legs. He drank three bottles of the yoghurt he'd pinched.

*Nothing like hiding in a toilet again, Rémy Dupree Rush. Like you didn't do enough of that in grade school.*

He squelched back the threatening tears. He'd grieve for all that he'd lost when he figured out all that he'd lost.

'The Victoria and Albert Museum is now open for visitors,' announced a polite recording.

Rémy climbed off the cistern, flipped his guitar case over his shoulder, rinsed the three empty yoghurt bottles in hot water and used a paper towel to pick them up and toss them in the bin. He didn't think the police had his fingerprints yet, but there was no point in being stupid.

Spotting a rambunctious school group filing up the stairs from the main entrance and gathering near the gift shop, Rémy slid among them, taking advantage of an ambivalent chaperone and a flustered teacher with too many tickets to give out.

'Sir! Young man!'

Rémy instinctively shoved his hand into his pocket and fingered his harmonica. Another busload of visitors was swarming the entrance. Too many people to control.

'Sir!' said the guard, jogging a little to catch up. 'I'm afraid you'll need to leave your guitar case in the cloakroom. We don't allow backpacks or any bulky bags in the museum.'

Relief flooded Rémy. He didn't want to be separated from his possessions, but at least he hadn't been rumbled.

His stomach growled as he deposited his guitar case at the cloakroom, the words on the museum map in his hands swimming across the page. It was difficult to concentrate with sleep and hunger and sorrow all competing for attention. The yoghurts he'd pilfered had only teased his appetite into thinking something more substantial was on its way. He was almost down to his last few coins, but if he didn't get some food soon, he'd let his guard down and his search would be over.

The Moor would have to wait.

# 40.

# A CABINET OF CURIOSITIES

The bluebottles swarming in and out of the cracks and crevices in the door began to slow in their frenzy, dropping one by one on to the stoop.

'They're dying,' said Matt, poking a finger into their fat carcasses. 'But not of starvation, that's for sure.'

Em had no desire to get any closer than she already was. She took out her sketchpad and a pencil and quickly drew a way into the shop.

A knife of light, like a laser, cut a hole around the lock. Matt reached his hand inside and unlatched the rear door. They stepped over the dying bluebottles and paused for a moment, listening.

'No alarm,' said Em.

Matt closed the door behind them.

'Maybe there's something inside this place that means they don't need one.'

'And thank you for that. You always know how to make a girl feel safe.'

Em tore up her sketch. In a snap of a second, the door restored itself to its original form.

Matt took off his shades and let his eyes adjust. 'Stay close.'

'Oh, I am,' said Em, grabbing the hem of his canvas jacket.

They made their way through what looked once to have been a kitchen and scullery area but now served as storage. Crates lay toppled to one side, some with the straw and the packing materials oozing out of their sides, others torn open and emptied completely. Everything was covered in dead or dying flies.

*Someone was looking for something.*

*I hope it was a can of Raid.*

The low buzzing sound they'd both heard from outside was louder in the shop itself.

'Jesus Christ!' Matt blurted.

Em dropped her grip from Matt's jacket and covered her mouth with her hands. They both stood with their backs to the wall and stared at the remains of a man in a navy pea coat stuck to the floor with a thick, greenish-yellow substance like putrid honey. Thousands of bluebottles were swarming out of the wet mass that had been his abdomen.

Averting their eyes, the twins stepped quickly and carefully round the corpse. It was impossible not to gag. To take her mind off the horror, Em busied herself clicking pictures of the strange, fly-ridden interior with her flip-phone. What was this place? Maybe Vaughn would know more when she showed him the images.

Matt was in the darkest corner of the shop, examining an old cabinet with brass handles and a hundred tiny drawers.

*There's something behind this cabinet, Em.*

*Like what?*

*I don't know, but I can see air coming through the back.*

'Of course you can, Superman,' Em mumbled to herself.

It took the twins ten minutes to find the trick access to the cabinet. All the drawers in the cabinet itself were empty, so they switched their attention to the heavily laden bookcase beside it. They emptied the shelves from the bottom up, feeling, pressing, twisting all the while. On the top shelf, Matt reached for a scroll fastened with a buckled leather strap. He pulled the buckle.

*Click.*

The back of the cabinet slid open smoothly, revealing what looked like a steel-lined panic room about as big as a walk-in closet. A red, velvet-cushioned throne chair sat against the far wall. The carcasses of three fleshy flies were pressed into the seat cushion.

'I saw a movie like this once,' said Matt, walking into the room and running his hands over the gleaming steel walls. 'A thief hides in a panic room so as not to get caught. There's a two-way mirror and he witnesses a murder.'

'Is it murder by flies?' said Em, swatting two bluebottles flying feebly at her neck.

Matt pushed his hands against the ceiling, feeling the steel flex under his palms.

'These walls are too thin for a panic room. I think there's something behind them. Come in here and help me.'

'You're not getting me in there,' said Em at once. 'Even without that dead body, this place is freaking me out. The air feels different. Not musty, but... tragic. Like it's left over from some really bad stuff in the past.'

Matt suddenly slid a panel open in the ceiling, revealing a plate with two silver buttons on it. Em's eyes widened.

'Don't touch those buttons!'

The words left her lips at the same time Matt hit one of the buttons.

The entire room dropped through the floor and disappeared.

# 41.

## INSIDE THE V&A

With the cafeteria wall behind him, and a broad, studious-looking guy with an Afro sipping an espresso in front of him for cover, Rémy wolfed down two egg sandwiches and two glasses of milk. The combination of carbs and protein would tide him over for a while. This was something else he'd learned from his homelessness: the all-consuming nature of hunger.

The espresso-drinking guy in front of Rémy got up to leave. Rémy noticed the lanyard dangling around his neck. The name on the lanyard read 'Mingus Franklin'.

'Your parents were jazz lovers, sir,' Rémy said, unable to help himself. 'Right?'

A wide smile split the man's brown face. 'It was a big name for a child, but thankfully I have grown into it,' he said in a deep bass voice. 'Are you a musician?'

Rémy nodded. 'Guitar. Horn too, and some harmonica.'

Mingus Franklin whistled. 'That's a whole lot of music.'

'Do you work here?' Rémy asked.

'I'm one of the curators on the new exhibition of Renaissance portraits we have running. It's well worth a visit. Some of the portraits have never been seen in the UK before.'

Rémy's heart leaped. Finally, a break.

'You wouldn't by any chance know anything about the Moor of Cadiz?' he blurted.

# 42.

# INTO THE WARDROBE

Em gazed into the black hole where the lift had been. The ceiling of the steel room was camouflaged to match the base of the cabinet.

*Matt! Matt! Can you hear me?*

The base of the cabinet shot upwards and Matt reappeared, legs crossed, sitting on the throne chair.

'Get in, Em,' he said. 'You need to see what's underneath this shop.'

'I'm not getting in there.'

'Don't argue,' said Matt.

He pulled her into the lift and hit the button again. The lift plummeted like a ride at a carnival. Em's stomach somersaulted. She slammed onto her knees as it came to a sudden pinpoint stop.

Another set of doors slid open, revealing what looked like a nineteenth-century drawing room. An uncomfortable-looking loveseat with a curved back embedded with lots of pearl buttons stood against a wall covered with blue and yellow flocked wallpaper in a tulip and willow pattern. The loveseat was facing a freestanding, triptych mirror and a double portrait of two men, one sitting and one standing. An open wardrobe stuffed with clothes stood to the left of the mirror with a wooden tailor's block in front. A table next to a small sink was neatly laid out with bricks of soap, a set of ivory brushes, bottles of creams and lotions, two vials of perfume, cotton pads, and a straight razor.

Em ran her hands across the delicate wall covering. 'This is original William Morris paper,' she said. 'This room's been here for a long time.'

'Big-time neat freak or what?' said Matt. 'Look how perfectly lined up and evenly spaced the items on that table are. All the pots and vials are in descending order of size.'

Em rifled through the wardrobe. She lifted out a red coat with gold brocade and a black frock coat with tails.

'A redcoat's uniform from the American Revolutionary War,' she said. 'And a nineteenth-century opera coat. There are other costumes in here too, dating back years by the looks of them.'

'Creepy portrait,' Matt said. 'Don't you think?'

Em looked back at the double portrait. A surge of sheer terror charged through her bones.

'Do you feel that, Matt?'

Matt's vision blurred and his eyes began to tear uncontrollably. He nodded and took a step back from the painting. Em looked more closely.

The wave of terror she felt was emanating from both figures in the double portrait, but it was stronger and more malevolent from the older man seated on a throne-like chair in the centre of the image. An open roll-top desk stood between the two figures. The desk was cluttered with items that Em knew from her art history studies represented the passions and characteristics of the sitters: pages of fluttering sheet music caught beneath a violin for their love of music, a cornucopia bursting with ripe fruit and a dripping flagon of wine for their appreciation of life's pleasures. There was also an upside-down wooden globe and a shepherd's compass lying on its side, these last two puzzled Em. When the items were placed the right way round in a painting, they represented the adoration of Christ and the spread of Christianity.

She'd never seen them inverted before. Two scrolls tied with shimmering twine sat next to a strange-looking owl with lidless eyes, which seemed to be staring out at Em. A golden tablet the size of a small book, with strange glyphs etched on it, rested on the seated man's thigh. Em had no clue what that stood for.

'It looks like a Holbein,' Matt said. 'It's an almost identical composition to his painting in the National Gallery, *The Ambassadors*.'

'I can feel its malevolence,' said Em.

The image of the second figure was unfinished, a tall, slim, slightly blurred silhouette of soft colours and hazy lines filling the space. The telltale pale blue light of an animation pulsed like a soft strobe around the border of the canvas.

'I don't think Caravaggio is the only person loose from his art,' said Em.

She glanced at her brother. Matt had pushed his shades up into his hair and was wiping his face with his untucked T-shirt. His eyes were snapping through every colour in the spectrum as if someone was pointing a remote at them.

'For God's sake,' she said sharply. 'Turn away from that painting!'

Keeping a safe distance, she took a quick video of the double portrait, making sure the images captured the pale blue light of its animation and the details of all the objects on the desk.

'It's like every horror movie we've ever watched,' said Matt, fumbling to get his shades out of his hair. 'All we need now is for the lift to shoot back up to the shop and trap us down here.'

It did.

'I knew I shouldn't have said that,' said Matt as he and Em stared in dismay at the closed lift doors. 'We need to get out of here. Draw something!'

'No time,' said Em helplessly. 'The lift is going to come down at any second.'

'I guess we have to do this the old-fashioned way,' said Matt. He yanked open the wardrobe doors. 'Get inside, quick.'

The twins threw themselves as far back into the wardrobe as possible, pushing through the clothes. Matt backed in on top of Em, scrambling to pull the wardrobe door closed behind him.

*Where are you now, Mr Tumnus?*

*That would be funny if it wasn't so terrifying, Matt. Move your leg, will you? It's stabbing my kidney.*

They both heard the lift start its descent.

*Feel free to draw us out of here, Em!*

Em started drawing as fast as she'd ever done in her life. Matt used his body to shield her sketchpad, to hide any giveaway explosion of light, as the lift door opened with a hiss. Two sets of footsteps exited the lift. One set headed across the stone floor towards the loveseat, but the other walked directly towards the wardrobe.

*Any time now, Em!*

A hand grasped the wardrobe's handle, turning it slowly. Em sensed a terrible bloodlust coming from the wardrobe door as she shaded the last part of her drawing.

The twins tumbled out of the back of the wardrobe, landing in three feet of soft snow.

'You have got to be kidding,' Matt said, clocking the wintry forest scene and a lamp post in the clearing up ahead.

'If you go on about Mr Tumnus moments before I start drawing,' said Em a little grumpily, 'what do you expect me to come up with?'

'Somewhere warmer than Narnia,' Matt growled. 'My feet are freezing.'

They waited ten minutes with the snow swirling around them. Then, cautiously, they climbed back inside the rear of the wardrobe, where Em tore up her drawing. Matt pressed his eye to the crack in the wardrobe door.

'He's gone into the painting,' he said. 'I think the coast is clear.'

Climbing out of the wardrobe, the twins stared warily at what was now a large, square painting of two men, one sitting and one standing. Just like his hazy silhouette, the standing figure was tall and slim, legs spread, head tilted back, eyes forward, a facial expression suggesting curiosity, intelligence and something else. Cunning.

A bluebottle fly buzzed lazily on the top of the gilt frame. Matt lifted a scattering of torn paper from the floor, and pieced it together.

'If this painting does have something to do with Conjurors and the Camarilla,' he said, 'they have Animare helping them. Someone drew that guy back into the portrait.'

It was clear from the way the figures were positioned that the seated man, soft and rounded and dressed in richly embroidered blue robes with pointed satin slippers, was the more powerful of the two. He was in stark contrast to the slim grace of the freshly returned figure who was wearing a red velvet frock coat and gold slippers. Three fingers were missing from his right hand.

Em shivered. 'I don't like the look of either of them,' she said. 'We really need to get out of here.'

The lift had never felt so loud. The twins left the emptied bookshelves as they were, horribly aware that the scattered books had already broadcast their break-in.

'Close your eyes if you want,' Matt said. 'We're leaving the same way we came in.'

Em squeezed her eyes shut, unwilling to revisit the flyblown corpse, as Matt guided her back through the shop. The sudden sense of her brother's surprise and relief made her open them again.

Everything was immaculate. Mary Poppins had clearly been working overtime. Not a bluebottle or a desiccated body in sight.

# 43.

# EXIT THE BUILDING

'*The Moor of Cadiz*,' said Mingus Franklin.

They had stopped in front of a painting the size and shape of a front door. In the painting, the Moor was standing under a set of ornate arched columns on a flight of sandy stone steps with what looked like a mosque or a palace behind him, the perspective of the architecture calling attention to his height and build. Large baskets filled with fruit, vegetables and spices sat in a row on the step beneath him, symbols of his great wealth.

For Rémy, the man himself was a lot more impressive than his fruit and veg. His layers of white robes were cinched at his waist by a broad leather belt studded with silver, two swords sheathed at his sides. Criss-crossing his chest were two more belts with a variety of other knives of varying shapes and sizes tucked beneath them. He was wearing a yellow turban whose tail wrapped across his mouth and neck, leaving only his dark, penetrating eyes visible. A small sign beside the painting read: 'On loan from the Museo Nacional del Prado, Madrid.'

'He looks like a bad-ass,' said Rémy in awe.

'Little is known about him except that he was wealthy, perhaps the last Caliph to remain in Grenada. We can see he was a patron of the arts, well educated. He loved music.'

'How do you know?' The curator pointed out a beautiful lute propped up against one of the arches in the painting.

'The painting tells us quite a lot,' Mingus went on. 'It's clear from the fruits and spices by his feet that he traded widely with Asia and Europe. As a well-educated man, he will have spoken multiple languages. The term "Renaissance Man" would be just about perfect to describe him.'

Under heavy glass in a case next to the painting sat two rows of swords and knives sitting on velvet pads. Rémy stared. They matched the weapons in the portrait.

'Those were found in the ruins of a palace near Seville, during an archaeological dig in the sixties,' explained the curator. 'We know they belonged to him because of the crest.'

Rémy's stomach flipped as the taste of his egg sandwiches made a return because the design on the tip of the knife blades in both the case and the portrait matched the mark on the back of his neck.

'It's an unusual crest,' Rémy managed to say. 'Isn't it?'

'The Moor was an unusual man. He was one of the few Caliphs who remained after the Moors were expelled from Spain in 1492. He fought valiantly for his people and later was recognized by Queen Isabella as a "true Spaniard". And then there was his great personal tragedy: the loss of his only son.'

'His son died?'

'We have a letter dated from the early sixteenth century that tells us the Moor's son just disappeared one day. Was never seen again. According to this account, the Moor was never the same man again. He secluded himself from the world. We believe the Moor left Spain not long after, a broken man, never to return.'

Words in Latin were lettered in gold across the bottom of the frame. Rémy's pulse raced as he read them: *Musica vivificat mortuos*. 'Music gives life to the dead.' He knew this phrase. The words were scribbled in his mother's journal, over and over again, page after page.

Something made Rémy look up. A guard was staring at him, putting his radio to his mouth.

Instinct kicked in. Rémy broke into a sprint, away from the startled curator, hurling himself through the emergency exit as the alarms started screaming. The same polite recording voice of earlier that morning began to speak.

'Please exit the building. Do not use the lifts. Do not panic. Please exit the building.'

## 44.

# MAKING TRACKS

Matt stayed in the shadows of the buildings as they walked along St Martin's Lane towards the church, shades firmly on his nose. Then, without any warning, he stopped and sat on a small wall in front of a boutique selling hats. He took out his phone and started texting feverishly.

Em frowned. 'You never text anyone.'

*I'm not texting. Sit next to me and act interested.*

*That'll be a stretch.*

Em sat down and pretended Matt's phone was the most interesting thing in London, listening carefully to her brother's voice in her head.

*Don't look, but we're being followed.*

Em looked.

*I said DON'T look. You are such a tool!*

*Sorry. You mean that girl over by Starbucks?*

Matt gave slight nod. *She's been on us since we left the shop.*

Now that Matt had pointed it out, Em could feel the girl's gaze like someone pressing fingers into her temples.

*Do you think she's one of the bad guys?*

Matt lifted his shades. His kaleidoscopic eyes were troubled. *I don't know.*

Em glanced at the girl again – only to see her hurrying away.

*Shit, she knows she's been seen.*

*Follow her!*

Em was already on her feet, close behind Matt.

She's heading for the Tube.

They ducked down the stairs and into the brightly lit tunnel beneath the Strand, pushing through the turnstiles, their eyes trained on the girl as she hurried ahead of them. They ran down the escalators, through more tunnels – on to a platform where a train stood waiting.

'Faster!' Matt ordered, breaking into a sprint. 'I want to ask her a few questions.'

'I'm going as fast as I can!' Em gasped.

The twins threw themselves through the closing doors of the carriage, one car away from the girl. Every now and then, the girl glanced in their direction, then looked back. Em had the sudden impression that she wanted them to follow her.

Westminster, St James's, Sloane Square, the District Line Tube rattled underground and overground, twisting and squealing on its tracks. When it reached South

Kensington, the girl glanced in the twins' direction again – then darted off the train.

'Excuse me, sorry…'

Matt pulled Em off the train and up the steps into the ticket hall. The girl was already halfway up the steps, her dark hair billowing around her shoulders. The twins did their best to keep her in their sights, but it was a warm autumn day in the heart of the city and it was as if the whole world had descended on London's cafés and restaurants.

Matt swore, looking left and right. 'I think she went that way…'

The moment they hit the Cromwell Road, Em ground to a halt, reeling from an overwhelming sense of fear. She looked round, feeling disorientated and a little sick. All thoughts of the girl were forgotten.

Matt glanced at her. 'What just happened?'

'I just got this awful feeling, Mattie…'

'Where from?' Matt asked, his voice urgent. 'A person? A place? Can you tell?'

'It came from over there.'

Em pointed to the wide entrance of the Victoria and Albert Museum.

# 45.

# LET ME GO

Rémy fled from the stairwell on the first floor of the Victoria and Albert Museum when he heard footsteps coming fast behind him. He cut through a long hallway, ducking among the statues to avoid the clusters of anxious visitors jostling their way to the emergency exits. The alarm was loud, the flashing lights bright, and both were making his eyes water. The golden tablet bounced against his breastbone, its vibrations thrumming.

*Run, Rémy. Run!*

He skidded into an empty lift and hit the button for the top floor. He gripped his harmonica and waited.

The doors opened on two people: male and female around his own age. Rémy flattened himself to the back of the lift with a gasp and reached for the button again.

'Out you come,' said the boy, grabbing Rémy by the scruff of his T-shirt.

Rémy pivoted in panic and threw a punch. The guy ducked, but Rémy's fist caught him on his chin, sending his shades flying. The girl raised her hand and effortlessly caught the shades mid-air, tossing them back to her partner.

'Chill, dude,' said the boy, rubbing his chin and repositioning his shades. 'We're here to help.'

Rémy hit out again, but this time the girl twisted his arm in a hold he couldn't shake. 'Who the hell are you? Let me go. *Let me go…*'

'Let's just say, my brother and I are a lot like you, and we want to help,' she said. 'And unless you want to be arrested and locked up, or forced to answer a lot of questions about how you disappeared into that statue, I'd suggest you stop fighting us.'

The girl was striking in an intense kind of way, pale skin with brilliant green eyes.

She projected an aura that screamed 'I could kill you with a look'. Her brother needed to cut his hair, shave and maybe ditch the shades. Oddly, Rémy didn't feel threatened by either of them. Instead, he felt a wave of calm emanating from them both.

'The Professor does that,' he said cautiously. 'In my head, he does the same thing. Are you like him?'

Em turned to her brother. 'You heard of a Professor?'

'Nope.'

She turned back to Rémy. 'Tell us about him later. I'm Em, he's Matt. And right now, we'd like to rescue you.'

Shouting and stomping feet could be heard in the stairwell and a swarm of cackling, cracking radios.

'Rémy Dupree Rush,' said Rémy. 'Whatever you plan to do, now would be a good time.'

Matt grabbed Em and Em grabbed Rémy, pulling him across the gallery to a shadowy corner to stand inexplicably in front of a seventeeth-century painting of a girl at a desk.

'Don't we need a door?' Rémy asked, looking over his shoulder.

'Where we're going,' quipped the boy, 'we don't need doors.'

Rémy could hear the mob crashing into the room behind them. His decision to trust these guys suddenly felt like the worst decision he'd ever made. He dimly registered the fingers of the boy – Matt? – flying across a sketchpad, bringing to life the picture hanging on the wall.

Rémy's skin tingled, his limbs turned to rubber, his heart flipped and his gut rolled. He thought his bones were dissolving and his head exploded with flashes of colour and light. It was like the guy was conjuring with a pencil.

Ah.

# 46.

# TOO MUCH AWESOME

A girl in a heavy satin dress stood up from behind a desk to greet the twins and Rémy as they tumbled out from behind the heavy curtains in her chambers.

'Thank heavens for a break in routine,' she said. 'I have not had many travellers recently and my fingers are sore and in need of rest. Are you from Orion?'

'You're aliens?' asked Rémy.

*He's an idiot.*

*He's adorable.*

'Not that kind of Orion,' said Em aloud. 'It's an organization that helps and protects people with… well, with supernatural abilities.'

Rémy rubbed the back of his neck.

'No shit. Sorry, miss,' he added, ducking his head in embarrassment at the girl settling back on her stool and adjusting her wide brocade skirts.

'Are you in pursuit of the one who's stealing our instruments?' asked the girl.

Em and Matt exchanged looks.

*Caravaggio mentioned that.*

'What do you know about these missing instruments?' Matt asked aloud.

'I've heard rumours from another traveller through my painting,' said the girl. She blushed prettily.

'Caravaggio,' the twins guessed in unison.

'What have you heard?' asked Em.

The young woman clasped her hands on her lap.

'Many alarming things. But one hardly knows what to believe with you Animare.'

'What's an Animare?' asked Rémy.

'We use our imaginations to bring drawings to life,' said Em.

'How come I've never heard of you guys?'

'It's one of our rules,' said Matt, sweeping his hair back from his face. 'Don't get noticed.'

'The force is strong with this one,' said Em, smiling at Matt and then Rémy. 'If not you wouldn't have survived fading with us.'

'Whoa,' said Rémy. 'That fading thing… it might have killed me?'

'I don't think you'd have died exactly,' said Em.

'Are you kidding me?'

The girl cleared her throat delicately.

'As I understand it, the villain is looking for a particular instrument hidden in a painting. I suppose he'll know it when he finds it. In the meantime, we must all sit here and worry that our instruments will be stolen next.'

Rémy thought about his mother's journal. Certain things were beginning to make sense.

'You know what she's talking about,' Em said, focusing her green eyes on him. 'I can feel it coming off you in waves.'

'Yes,' Rémy said simply. 'I do.'

'Do you know about the Camarilla?' Matt asked.

Rémy shivered and nodded. 'Yes.'

'Are they the ones looking for this instrument?'

Rémy nodded again. 'I think so.'

'Why?' asked Em.

That, Rémy couldn't answer.

'We need to get you somewhere safe,' said Matt. 'Then you need to tell us what you were doing in that shop off the Strand yesterday.'

Em pointed at a small painting above the girl's desk. 'We'll use that to fade back to Scotland,' she said.

Rémy raised his hands. 'I can't go to Scotland,' he said.

'What's wrong with Scotland?' Matt snapped.

'I need to get my guitar case. It's still in the museum coat check. My mom's journal is in the case. It explains… a lot.'

Matt sighed, shoving his shades on to the top of his head.

'Jesus, dude,' said Rémy. 'What's wrong with your eyes? That must hurt.'

'Only when I get into seventeeth-century brawls.'

'My brother can time travel with his eyes,' Em explained.

Rémy laughed loud, a deep throaty laugh that lit up his whole face.

'Oh my God, there's just too much awesome in that sentence for me to handle.'

Matt grinned. He couldn't help himself. There was something appealing about Rémy Dupree Rush.

'How long have you guys had your powers?' Rémy asked.

'Forever,' said Em. 'But we never really did anything with them until we were nine or ten. What about you? How did you escape through the statue?'

'I sang Puccini,' said Rémy. 'My mom has... had a record.'

'Had?' Em said.

'She died.'

Em touched Rémy's arm. 'I'm sorry,' she said. 'We lost our dad when we were younger.'

They shared a silent moment, the air heavy with feeling.

'I'm a Conjuror,' Rémy said after a while. 'When I sing or play, I can change the structure of objects and I can create new things... And, according to my mother's journal, I'm the only one who can save the world from the rise of the Second Kingdom.'

# 47.

# PUTTING IT TOGETHER

Annie Dupree Rush's bulging journal resembled the walls Rémy had seen when he had burst into her room the day she died. Pulling it carefully from its padded bag as he stood alone at a London post-office box opened by the small key she'd slipped over his neck. Photos, articles torn from magazines and scribbled sketches had fallen from the journal's pages when he opened it up for the very first time. Sheet music, riffs and choruses from songs, family trees and timelines, phrases from concertos and song cycles – everything was stuffed between its word-packed pages. And everywhere, the scrawled phrase *musica vivificat mortuos*, with furious underlines.

*Music gives life to the dead.*

Rémy took the journal from its hiding place inside the lining of his guitar case and placed it on the table at the church for Vaughn, Matt and Em to see.

'The man… the thing that murdered my mom and my Tia Rosa called himself Don Grigori. This is what he was looking for.'

Vaughn whistled. 'This is a lot of research,' he said. 'You say you'd never seen it before you took it from that locker?'

'I saw her writing in it sometimes when I'd come home from school, but she'd hide it as soon as I walked in the door,' Rémy said. 'I thought it was just a diary, a way for her to make sense of the voices, the melodies and the strange noises in her head. Every Christmas I'd buy her a new one, and every Christmas she'd thank me and then put it in a drawer and never use it. I think she was afraid that if she began anew, she'd lose track of what she'd already discovered. It was as if her journal was holding her thoughts in place.'

Vaughn pulled a colour printout from among the pages. It showed a double portrait of two wealthy men, one sitting and one standing. The man on the left was tall and long-limbed, his arm and what remained of his fingers draped gracefully over the back of a mahogany throne chair. The seated man was red-faced and well fed, clothed in rich robes.

Rémy saw Em and Matt exchange a glance.

Vaughn noticed too. 'What aren't you telling me?' he said.

Em looked uncomfortable. 'We saw that painting,' she said. 'At Old Worm's yesterday.'

Rémy rose to his feet. 'It was there? I searched for it everywhere!'

Matt explained about finding the lift and the secret room. About the portrait, how it had only contained one man when they had hidden in the wardrobe, and two when they had re-emerged.

Pulling the golden tablet from around his neck, Rémy slammed it on the table beside the journal.

'Mom gave me this before she died,' he said, running his fingertip over the strange glyphs etched on its surface. 'It took me to the shop. It told me where to look. I just didn't look hard enough.'

'What did your mother want you to do with the painting?' Vaughn asked.

'Destroy it,' said Rémy bitterly. 'And find the Moor, whoever the hell he is.'

'I'm guessing you haven't found him yet,' said Em.

'Not unless you count the portrait of the Moor of Cadiz, hanging in the Victoria and Albert Museum. But how could it be him? How's it possible that a 500-year-old guy in a painting could be of any help to me?'

Em and Matt exchanged glances again. This time Vaughn joined them.

'Enough with the all-knowing looks,' said Rémy in frustration. 'What is going on?'

'Sit,' said Matt, pushing a desk chair over to Rémy. 'It's possible, because he may not exactly be 500 years old.'

'When Animare fade in and out of art, time, as we measure it, freezes,' Vaughn explained. 'Inside a painting, it can feel as if hours have passed, days even, but when we emerge it may only have been seconds.'

'So what you're saying,' said Rémy, doing his best to understand, 'is that an Animare could go into a painting and stay there for centuries before he or she emerges again?'

'An Animare, yes,' said Matt. 'And maybe someone or something with an Animare's help.'

Em suddenly jumped up from the table. Rémy watched, startled, as a red balloon floated out of the Banksy mural in the Plexiglas box behind them and up to the rafters.

'Excitement, Em. Down a notch,' warned Matt.

'Sorry.' Em sat back down. 'If an Animare helped the guy at Old Worm's get back into the painting, maybe an Animare is helping the Moor too.'

'It's possible,' said Vaughn, shaking his head. 'Orion has been spread pretty thin in recent years trying to monitor groups like the Hollow Earth Society and their continued attempts to undermine the authority of the Councils.'

'Whoever is helping this Grigori creature,' said Rémy, flipping the pages back in his mother's journal, 'I think my mom may have gotten in his way once before, and…'

The words caught in his throat because saying them aloud made it real.

'And… I think they killed my dad to try to stop her.'

# 48.

# THIS HAPPENED

It had taken Rémy several days to make sense of significant parts of his mother's journal, tucked up in his small sleeping space in the Professor's tent. Memories from that day in the plantation museum shifted and re-shaped themselves into a more coherent whole. The painting. The tall man carrying the small blue fan because of the suffocating heat. The terrible screeching of brakes... the squeal of tyres... the sickening smash of metal on flesh... his mother's horrified screams.

'Mommy, I need to go!'

'A minute, RD,' Mommy said, copying furiously from a book that smelled like wet dog. 'Can you hold it for just a minute longer, baby boy?'

But Rémy had to pee now. And he was not a baby boy. He was a big boy. He could do this on his own. He darted away. But he was quickly lost.

As he wandered among shelves of cardboard boxes and piles of brown files held together with elastic bands, he looked up and saw a blinking red exit sign. But instead of the hallway to the restrooms as he had hoped, the door opened at the top of a flight of narrow iron stairs. The stairs led down to a storage room cluttered with old furniture that stank even worse than his mother's books. There was a couch that looked like a bed, a table stacked with chairs and a filthy claw-footed bathtub. Rémy had felt a flash of hope. Maybe there was a toilet too.

He toddled deeper into the space. A terrible noise flashed through his head, blinding him with pain. Reeling with shock, Rémy tripped over a rolled-up rug to land on his stomach behind a sideboard.

From his position on the floor, he noticed a pair of legs ending in a pair of shiny black shoes. He watched, mesmerized, as the man with the shiny shoes, a notepad folded under his left arm, offered his right hand to a tall skinny man who was climbing out of a painting.

Rémy scrambled to his feet, banging his head on the sideboard. He charged back through the stacks, knocking over boxes and screaming at the top of his lungs. But the man from the painting had caught him at the bottom of the iron staircase.

'He floated in front of me, holding one of those plastic battery-operated fans to his face,' Rémy said now. 'I thought it was strange because I was freezing cold. Next thing I heard my mom singing in my head as she scooped me up in her arms. The man was gone. I remember... '

Rémy let his tears flow freely. 'I remember whispering in my mom's ear that I was sorry I'd wet my pants and that please would she not tell my dad.'

# 49.

# FAST LEARNERS

Em was shivering, even though the sun was streaming in through the stained-glass window above their heads.

'I think we all need a cup of tea,' said Matt.

'I'd rather have a latte,' said Rémy, wiping his eyes with the heels of his hands. 'Haven't had one since I've been on the streets.'

When Matt returned with a tray, Rémy and Vaughn had shifted to the couch and Em was cross-legged on the reading chair.

Rémy stared at the musical note Matt had drawn in the foam of his latte. 'Is this real or supernatural?'

'I'm insulted,' said Matt, grinning. 'I do have one or two normal talents, you know.'

'Tell us what you can about the men in the painting, Rémy,' said Vaughn, rubbing the stubble on his chin.

'The man on the left was once the most famous *castrato* in history, Don Grigori de Cordoba,' Rémy said with effort. 'The other man was his patron, Cardinal Rafael Oscuro, a Grand Inquisitor of the Spanish Inquisition.'

'Whoa, hold the bus,' said Matt. 'A *castrato*? You mean he had his junk cut off so he could sing like a girl?'

'Not exactly. His endocrine duct was severed, which meant his testicles shrivelled up and his voice stayed high. Women were banned from singing in Vatican choirs, and the Pope needed *castrati* to sing the soprano parts during mass.' Rémy's face twitched. 'In Spain, butchers did the procedures because they were skilled at preparing pigs for market. Pigs' testicles still are a delicacy in lots of places.'

'I think I just threw up in my mouth,' said Matt.

'Making boys *castrati* was also a way for many poor families to curry favour with the Vatican and its cardinals,' Vaughn added. 'They sold their boys to the Catholic Church.'

'That's terrible,' said Em. 'The Church has done a lot of nasty stuff.'

Vaughn studied the portrait again. 'This was painted when, early sixteenth century?' he said. 'And you all say one of these men was out of the painting?'

'Don Grigori,' said Rémy. His face hardened. 'He killed my mother and Tia Rosa four weeks ago, and now he's after me. Apparently these two abominations in the portrait can't fulfil their destiny if I'm still alive.'

'What destiny?' asked Em.

'A lot of Mom's journal makes no sense to me,' Rémy admitted. 'She wrote in some kind of code. But in a few places she writes about a secret organization called the Camarilla's plans for something called the Second Kingdom, and that when it comes she writes that the "dead will rise and the fallen will rule". Their destiny must have something to do with this Second Kingdom.'

'Do you think these guys are the ones stealing instruments from paintings?' asked Em.

*Em!*

Startled by Matt's scream in her head, Em choked on her tea, spurting it out through her nose.

Vaughn held up his hands. 'What? Who told you instruments were being taken from paintings?'

'One of Vermeer's young women,' said Matt, covering for Em while she mopped tea from her cardigan. 'When we faded from the museum.'

Vaughn's eyes narrowed. 'Really? I've sent you both on precisely two uncomplicated missions,' he said. 'You're trainees. You remain on probation from the Council. You aren't supposed to be involved in cases like this.'

Em shrugged. 'What can I say? We're fast learners.'

Vaughn threw his hands in the air. 'Oh, for God's sake, tell me everything you know.'

# 50.

## ANNIE'S JOURNAL

The rustle of tree branches against the leaded glass windows of the church was like brushes on snare drums.

'Do you have any idea how unique you are, Rémy?' asked Vaughn.

'I don't know about unique,' said Rémy. *But I could tell you about lonely.*

Em was carefully sifting through Annie's journal, its leather-bound pages open on the makeshift coffee table. A handful of musical scripts were fastened together with paperclips, others were stapled or glued, but all were handwritten in thin letters that were a combination of cursive and printing.

'My mom's first journal entry after my dad's death was about the strange mark on the wrist of the hit-and-run driver who killed him,' said Rémy, leaning over the journal with Em. 'I saw it again on a guy in a blue coat at Old Worm's when he came at me with a Taser.'

'He sounds like the dead guy Em and I found today at the shop,' said Matt.

'Someone died?' asked Vaughn, half rising from the chair. 'What happened to the body?'

'The flies ate it,' said Em. 'There was nothing left.'

'Big bastards the size of your fist,' said Matt with a shudder.

'They're Don Grigori's,' said Rémy, bile rising in his throat at the thought of the flies doing the same to his mother and Tia Rosa.

Vaughn looked pale. 'This is very bad. Too many bodies and too many unknown factors. We need to get more help on this.' He glared at the twins. 'More experienced help.'

Rémy picked up the journal, rubbing his finger across the creases in the leather.

'My mom spent years digging through the archives trying to find out what that mark meant, and how it was related to the Conjuror's mark I bear on my neck and that she had on hers.'

'Can we see the mark?' asked Em.

Rémy slipped off his hood and turned his back to them. The pink puckered lines of the mark were clear and raised against his brown skin. 'My mom eventually found a similar mark mentioned in the papers of a slave ship that came to America a few years before the Atlantic slave trade began in full. She found out about it around the time she learned about the Camarilla protecting the creatures in the painting.'

He picked through the scraps and notes of the bulging book until he found the pages he was looking for. 'My mom copied these words into her journal from the letters that she found in the plantation archives. AB is the overseer, Alonzo Blue.'

**March 19, 2004: Notes from AB letter dated 1803 to his daughter in New Iberia.**

The first Conjuror came to America in a slave ship.

In 1797 a lone ship drifted up a tributary of the Mississippi. Alonzo Blue, overseer of the Dupree Plantation, spotted the two-decker bobbing in the choppy water. As word spread of the ship's strange arrival, the field slaves vanished into their damp huts, closed their shutters and shoved pellets of hardtack into their ears (see journal vol. 2 append. III, Dupree Family Archives, 1806). They could sense what was coming.

At dusk the voice of an angel singing a wordless aria could be heard, like the fluting sound of the breeze through the sugar cane, or the delicate notes of the harpsichord in the big house's front parlour. The music floated from the ship in a pulsing silver mist, above the moss-draped oaks, through the rubber trees dripping with wet lichen, dipping and darting across the indigo fields until it reached the party at the plantation house, where handsome

guests were sipping sweetened rum from tulip-
shaped glasses on the wide veranda.

At the cool touch of the mist, the guests' fingers
twitched, their limbs stiffened, their eyes fluttered
and their glasses fell to the wooden planks of the
porch. The women's ears trickled blood on to the
lace of their white cotton dresses. The men's collars
sliced into the throbbing veins in their necks.

The music stopped.

Out on the delta, the wind stilled and birds appeared
to perch on every part of the silent ship: ravens as
black as coal and as big as buzzards, like feathered
gargoyles on a floating cathedral.

There must'a been a bird for each slave's soul.
The ship looked at any moment like it might rise up
off the water and fly.

With his head throbbing from the music and
the mist, Alonzo Blue tucked a pistol into his
breeches, cloaked his body in sackcloth against the
mosquitoes, hooked his machete over his shoulder
and dragged the rowboat from the boathouse on to
the bayou.

The tall live oaks towered over him like giants
standing knee-deep in water, their branches scraping
the cloudless, starry sky. He lassoed his rope to an
iron ring on the side of the now silent, feathered ship
and hoisted himself on to the deck.

Every bird on the ship took flight.

Alonzo Blue saw the girl first, her hair shining like velvet in the moonlight. She was sitting on the deck naked except for a bloody sheet wrapped around her waist, the excess cloth gathered beneath her protruding belly. Like the blessed Virgin, she cradled her infant at her breast.

But it was the grotesque tableau laid out behind her that sent the overseer to the side of the ship, where he vomited into the water's murky depths.

A young man, a slave with the Conjuror's mark on his neck, had been drawn and quartered, each piece of him set out in its correct anatomical position, except for one part of him that had been shoved into his mouth.

There were no other survivors. The carcasses of fat bluebottle flies carpeted the deck.


The silence stretched as each of them finished reading the entry.

'That's horrible,' said Em at last.

'So you think you're descended from the baby?' said Matt at last.

'Yes,' said Rémy. 'According to the birth records for the plantation, Alonzo Blue persuaded the surviving family members on the plantation that he would take the slave girl for himself and raised her child as his own. According to my mom's research, in another letter she discovered, the child had the mark of the Conjuror. I think that's why I have the same name as the plantation: Dupree.'

'Because your mom and you are descendants of that slave girl,' said Em.

Remy nodded, unfolding a photocopy of a property deed that was tucked in a pocket at the back of the journal. 'A chunk of bayou belonging to the plantation was signed over to Alonzo Blue at the close of the eighteenth century. He lived well into old age.'

'Makes you wonder what else got off that boat, doesn't it?' said Em, thinking about the horror Blue witnessed on that slave ship.

'The passage your mom copied from the archives mentions flies,' Em said aloud. 'Flies seem to be Don Grigori's calling card, so I'm guessing he slaughtered the slaves.'

'This is 1797,' Vaughn pointed out. 'The only way Don Grigori could have been present would be if the painting had been cargo on the ship.'

'It was,' said Rémy. 'According to my mom's research, Alonzo Blue removed it from the ship along with a trunk of gold, jewels and silver from the hold. I think he must have stolen some of the gold and used it to buy the Dupree land a few years later when he could claim to have saved for it. The house he built still belongs to my family. But I don't think anyone understood what evil had been bound in the painting. The painting stayed in the plantation house until the Dupree line died years ago. Then it disappeared. My mom did her best to trace it, but... well. You know the rest.'

'This was your father's line or your mother's?' Vaughn asked.

'My mother's. My dad was from London,' Rémy said. 'They met at a concert when she was performing at the Royal Albert Hall.'

'If the portrait was in the plantation house collection from 1797 until twelve years ago,' said Em, working it out, 'what happened twelve years ago to set this all in motion?'

'I did,' said Rémy. 'When I fled from Don Grigori in the museum as a boy, he saw the mark on the back of my neck.'

Vaughn grabbed his phone and his jacket. 'I need to make some calls. Do not move. Any of you.'

When Vaughn was gone, Rémy tucked the journal and its contents back beneath the lining of his guitar case. He pulled on his hoodie, and then his jacket.

'Going somewhere?' asked Matt.

'My mom was a rare and special person, but all the music in her head and the knowledge she was gathering was too much for her.' Rémy's voice shook. 'It broke her mind and her heart. It came down to my Tia Rosa to raise me and do her best to protect both of us. Whatever these two creatures in that painting are planning, I'm going to stop them. I'd like your help, but if you can't give it, I'll understand. Either way, I'm not waiting around for the cavalry.'

'I think we know where that painting is,' said Matt, tugging his jacket from beneath his sleeping bag. 'Em and I could fade into it, inspirit Don Grigori and this Grand Inquisitor and bind them permanently into the portrait. How hard could it be?'

Vaughn came back into the room at that moment.

'Are you kidding me? You're seventeen years old,' he yelled. "You are not to have anything further to do with this. Am I clear?'

Matt looked mutinous.

'Am I clear?' Vaughn repeated. He and Matt glared at each other.

Em sat at the edge of the chair.

*Back off, Matt.*

'Sure, Vaughn,' said Matt finally. 'Whatever you say.'

Vaughn looked suspicious. 'I mean it.'

...when all the world dissolves,
And every creature shall be purified,
All place shall be hell that is not heaven.

*Dr Faustus*

# FIFTH MOVEMENT

# 51.

# HOT AS HADES

Seville's historic Giralda bell tower was the first thing the twins and Rémy noticed when they stepped from a private gallery to the cobbled central plaza. The scorching August heat was the second.

'Damn! It's hot,' said Rémy, fanning himself.

Matt looked at his phone. 'It's thirty-five degrees. High nineties Fahrenheit. Hot as hell, basically, and the valley is going to be worse.'

'I knew we should have changed before we left Scotland,' said Em.

'We didn't have time,' said Matt, ponytailing his hair. 'If we hadn't faded straightaway, Vaughn would have locked us all up until his other agents arrived. We were lucky we got out when we did.'

'I've got a little cash left from my busking,' said Rémy. 'I can help pay for some supplies at least.'

Em patted Rémy's arm. 'Keep your money. Matt and I still have most of our Orion cash. It's not as if fading cost us anything to get here.'

'Speak for yourself,' said Matt, rolling his neck muscles and flexing his fingers.

After a quick shopping spree at a tourist market on the other side of the square where they bought water, a box of granola bars, a map and a splashy-coloured summer dress for Em, one that went with her black boots, they rented a locker at the train station where they locked up their phones. If they were going to investigate this without Orion's help, they couldn't allow their phones to be tracked.

Em spread the map of the area out on a nearby bench.

'The village of Olivera is about 140 kilometres from here. No way are we hiking that in this heat. It'll take us days, and we don't have days. We need to find the painting before Vaughn or the Camarilla find us.'

'You're sure Olivera is the village in your mother's journal?' Matt checked.

'Positive,' said Rémy. 'The Grand Inquisitor's family owned all the land surrounding the village. My mom tracked the painting's provenance to a wealthy family living near the village.'

'A car?' suggested Em.

'We're not old enough to rent one,' Rémy pointed out.

Em pulled a sketchpad from her messenger bag and vanished round the corner. Five minutes later, she returned, waving a set of car keys in front of the two boys.

'Our carriage awaits,' she said.

Round the corner, in the station's loading zone, Em popped the boot on a shiny red Volkswagen Eos convertible. The twins tossed their backpacks inside. Rémy set his guitar case next to them.

'I've always wanted one of these,' said Em, patting the car as she slammed the boot and pulled open the driver's door.

Matt moved in front of her. 'No way. I'm driving. You're a maniac behind the wheel.'

'My animation,' said Em as she shoved him straight back. 'I'm driving.'

'Shotgun,' said Rémy, quickly jumping into the passenger's seat.

Matt had no choice but to fold himself, grumbling, into the narrow back seats.

If it hadn't been for the dark reasons behind this road trip, they might have actually enjoyed the journey. They decided to avoid the motorway, so their route took them deeper into the Spanish countryside. The landscape here was stunning, the red mountains dotted with castles, churches and rugged villages tucked into the side of the hills.

Rémy kept his eyes glued to his mother's journal, reading out bits he thought were relevant.

'According to this,' he said, 'the village we want is beyond this range of mountains.'

As she drove, Em's attention wandered away from Rémy's voice to other parts of his body. He was wearing a pair of Matt's Ray-Bans, and had rolled his T-shirt up to his shoulders. He was in fine shape. Em wondered if he worked out.

*If you wanted to look at him instead of the road, you should have sat back here. I've a fine view.*

*All you can see are his legs and his... Get out of my head, Mattie!*

'Did you hear anything I said?' asked Rémy.

Em blinked at Rémy. 'Sorry, what?'

Rémy looked at her. 'Are you guys telepathic? You both zoned out on me.'

'Bad twin habit,' said Matt, sitting up. 'Sorry.'

Rémy grinned. 'I noticed you doing it in Scotland. It must be cool.'

*Em wants to ki-iss you, Em wants to lo-ove you...*

'Sometimes it's a pain in the arse,' said Em, a little more loudly than normal. 'What were you saying?'

'I was saying, there's more about the Grand Inquisitor in Mom's journal than I thought. Mom used a musical cipher to code chunks of what she had written.' Rémy took off his shades and rubbed his eyes. 'The Professor helped me break it. In the late fifteenth century Cardinal Rafael Oscuro, Grand Inquisitor to the King and Queen of Spain, bought the village of Olivera and the remains of a Moorish castle on an outcrop of the mountain. He built his palace around the ruins of that castle to give himself extra protection from his growing number of enemies. Then, around 1510, the village, the land, castle and palace, everything was all suddenly deeded to the Trastámara family for very little money.'

'The Trastámara must be part of the Camarilla,' said Matt.

'1510 is around the time the portrait was painted,' Em commented, kicking the car into a lower gear as they climbed higher.

'Exactly. The Grand Inquisitor must have sold up and climbed into the painting to hide for a couple of hundred years.'

'But why?' asked Matt.

'Something big must have happened,' said Rémy.

Up ahead the road narrowed and got steeper. They all felt their ears pop. Suddenly the road opened up to a hairpin bend. Em braked hard, skidding the rear tyres.

'Let's try to get there in one piece, Em!' Matt shouted from the back.

'All right, that's enough!'

After two more tight curves and a hill that forced Em to keep her fingers on the handbrake for backup, they reached Olivera.

Every building and structure in the village was white, including a small church with tiled steps leading to a massive arched door. The church functioned as the tourist centre for the area. A café, a car-repair garage, a gallery and a taverna stood in a horseshoe in front of the church.

Em pulled the car over and parked next to a row of houses, indistinguishable from each other except for the bold colour of their doors. As she opened the car door, she blenched.

'God, what is that horrible smell?'

'What smell?' Matt jumped from the back of the car and stretched his arms and legs. 'I don't smell much of anything. Maybe the clay? Or something from the café?'

Em got out of the car and looked up at the church directly ahead. 'It's this place. It's foul. It smells like death and... I'm going to be sick.'

Em gagged and threw up in the gutter.

'Is she OK?' Rémy asked Matt in alarm.

'It's a thing. She'll be fine. She senses intense emotions from a place. Sometimes they can make her sick.'

After a few minutes, a bottle of water and a stick of gum, Em stood with the boys staring at a postcard-perfect place that was screaming in pain.

# 52.

# DRIVING WHILE INVISIBLE

The ruins of the castle and palace were visible on an outcrop of the hillside above the village. Shading his eyes, Matt could see the thin dirt trail they'd climbed, winding a path through the scrub.

'Probably take us around an hour to hike that path and get to that highest point,' he said, indicating a crag above the palace's broken walls.

Rémy laid a hand on Em's back. 'You OK to climb?'

Matt noticed how the touch of Rémy's hand brought a little colour back into Em's cheeks. 'Right now,' she said, 'I can't leave this place fast enough.'

They left the car parked in front of the café under the watchful eyes of a handful of locals, eating tapas and drinking red wine. Shouldering their backpacks, the three of them headed for the path.

It was a stiff climb. At what remained of the arched front entrance to the palace, they stopped for breath and looked back down along the dusty path towards the village. Two men from the taverna were standing out in the middle of the road, observing their progress.

'We're being watched,' said Rémy.

'We're probably the most interesting thing that's happened to this place in five centuries,' said Matt.

'Keep going. I want to get an overview from that crag,' said Rémy. 'We can climb round from the back.'

They hiked until it was clear they could no longer be seen from the village. They were soaked with sweat. The climb had taken them longer than they'd hoped. On the crag, they had a clear view of what remained of the palace and its gardens, with its broken statuary and its round reflecting pools long run dry. It was a dust bowl of yellow scrub brush, clusters of fat cacti, bulging agave plants popping with pink flowers and a few miniature palm trees.

The palace itself was an empty shell, though its former magnificence was clear from its outline. Pieces of inlaid decorative tiles remained in the sandstone walls, and beneath the foundation were the remains of a long narrow rectangular bath with one side still tiled in a red scarab design.

Everything was still. Too still.

'Have you noticed?' said Matt as they headed down towards the palace entrance. 'We've not seen a single creature since we left the village. No birds. No insects. Only a few shrubs and cacti.'

He felt his eyes twitching and watering. Trails of light

were shooting past his vision and he was finding it difficult to keep his balance.

'You need to do it soon,' Em said, noticing. 'Before it gets dark.'

Matt grimaced. 'I've never done it deliberately before. What if it doesn't work?'

'It'll work,' said Em with confidence.

'My sister,' said Matt, glancing at Rémy. 'Ever the optimist.'

'All we need are sketches of what you see. And whatever happens, don't get involved in the scene,' said Em. 'Promise. No matter what. Stay out of it.'

'Promise.'

*Mean it.*

*I mean it.*

They moved beneath the crumbling archway and walked quickly across the dried-up gardens, heading for what was left of the palace itself.

'I smell lilies,' said Em, jogging to catch up with the long strides of the two boys.

'I smell danger.' Rémy pointed to the distant dust trail of a vehicle heading up the road from the village. 'Something tells me they aren't driving this way for a chat.'

'I've an idea,' said Matt, ducking under a crumbled arched gateway in the wall. 'It might buy me some time so that I can concentrate on the past without the present interrupting.'

He swiftly outlined his plan.

'Are you sure?' asked Em.

'I hate to leave you.' Rémy glanced unhappily at the dust trail again. 'This is my fight after all.'

'It's our fight now,' said Matt. 'Go.'

Em gave a swift nod. Taking Rémy's hand, she dragged him back towards the archway and the dusty, curving road. To meet whoever was coming head on.

An old yellow Ford pick-up truck charged along the dusty road towards them. It was impossible to see who was behind the wheel, or how many were packed into its cab.

Em and Rémy stepped out into the road, waving at the truck to stop.

The truck skidded to the kerb in a cloud of dust. The engine idled for a second, then sputtered and died. No one jumped out.

'Can you see who's inside?' asked Rémy quietly as they approached the vehicle.

Em cupped her hands to her eyes. The glare from the setting sun was blinding. 'Something's wrong,' she said. 'I can't sense anything. I... it's like the truck's empty.'

Rémy slid his harmonica from his pocket, rolling it nervously in his hand.

'That's impossible. Someone has to be driving, right?' He squinted at the truck. 'Maybe it's an animation from someone like you.'

The cloud swirled around the cab. The silence stretched.

'I don't like this,' said Em. 'We should go back and get Matt.'

'Em, we can't. We have to let him finish what he's doing, or this whole trip is pointless. Let me try something.'

Watching the truck carefully, Rémy pulled Em off the dusty road and over to a scrub-filled ditch.

'I'm going to play. See if I can draw them out. Block your ears.'

Em inhaled and exhaled, closing her eyes and shoving her fingers in her ears.

'Go!'

Rémy put his harmonica to his lips. He began with a blues riff and then moved to a jaunty march, letting the music build. The music thickened into mist. With a flick of the wrist so fast that Em almost missed it, he blasted the truck with a fast screaming chord. The music swirled away into the trees, the notes caught in the branches for a beat, shaking the leaves before dispersing into the sky like embers from a dying fire.

The truck doors flew open and a man in jeans and a filthy white T-shirt rolled from the cab to the ground.

'I didn't mean to hurt him,' said Rémy breathlessly as Em ran to the man and kneeled to check his pulse.

'You didn't. He's been drugged. Something was controlling him as he drove—'

Em sensed the swarm before she saw it.

'It's trap, Rémy,' she shouted. 'Run!'

'I'm not leaving you here!'

A legion of fat flies rose from the bed of the truck. A tall man with curling blond hair and a tailored black suit floated in the midst of the thick, swarming mass, his thin fingers holding a pitch pipe at his lips.

Before Em could reach for her sketchpad or Rémy for his harmonica, Don Grigori began to play.

The wild, keening sound brought Em to her knees. The flies were on her immediately, filling her mouth and her mind. Her last thoughts were of Rémy watching her as if from behind a leaded-glass window, unable to reach her.

# 53.

# TURN ROUND

Matt had tucked himself into a cleft in the crumbling wall, his sketchpad resting on his knees. He was in the best position he could find. With the palace's cracked foundations, tiled remains of the baths and the stone pillars that had once held up the whole structure squarely in his sight, he began to draw.

He sketched the Grand Inquisitor's palace as he imagined it had once looked, filling in with smudges and shadows the weight of its walls and the grandeur of its balconies. He imagined the tiles in their full glory, the baths with their swirling pattern of red scarab beetles, yellows and blues bursting from the grey of his drawing, flashes of light and colour sparking from his charcoal as he drew.

He began to blink uncontrollably, the extra, thin shimmering membrane altering his vision. He blinked again, this time controlling how quickly it flicked across his vision. Blood, thick and red, was seeping through the cracks between the tiles like treacle. Matt saw a vast bath, filled with scarlet water that matched the scarab tiling, the naked limbs of a boy struggling against a man with the knife of a butcher, his apron spattered with blood...

Matt gagged and blinked, hard and fast.

He flipped to another sheet.

*Don't think about what you just saw. Don't think... Vomit later.*

His fingers danced across the paper as his imagination took full control. The palace began to emerge in its full Renaissance glory, as if he was watching a stop-motion film. And then the images all slowed to a shimmering halt, and sound, like that of a soprano's voice exploding with nails, fractured his consciousness.

Tears of blood fell from his eyes on to the paper. He blindly wiped them with the back of his hand, drawing, still drawing...

The ground shook with a deafening boom and the palace collapsed before Matt, a mass of rubble and rocks, its entire apron covered in red beetles twitching to their deaths.

A man in a brown skullcap, a tan tunic and green breeches with an artist's pouch over his shoulder appeared at the bottom of the rubble. Matt strained to see his face.

*Turn round! Turn round!*

The artist began to draw something on a piece of parchment. Steps burst into life, stretching up the palace wall to the first floor. Quickly, the artist began to climb, taking the steps two at a time, staying close to the wall, clearly afraid of being seen. Midway, he turned, as if he'd heard the sound of Matt's charcoal scratching across the paper.

*Got you!*

The image shimmered, changed. Matt blinked once, twice. The artist was now climbing back down the stairs clutching something beneath his arm, an expression of horror on his face. Matt felt fear and regret and resolve, then lost the connection as the artist erased his drawing and the stairs vanished into the dust.

A small black boy, dressed in a filthy sackcloth tunic, crawled out from a gap between two slabs of marble. Matt flipped to another page frantically and sketched him, capturing the outline of his face before the child, too, vanished.

A tall, black man covered in chalky dust now stood at the maw of the palace balcony. He stood erect, in spite of his shredded robes and what looked like a deep wound in his thigh, bound in a bloody yellow scarf. The man had knives tucked in bands of leather across his broad chest and a sword sheathed at his hip. The child that had crawled from between the marble slabs was in his arms. Keeping hold of his charge, the man leaped from the balcony and slid down the rubble, disappearing towards the edge of Matt's vision.

Matt sketched furiously, his fingers on fire, his imagination beginning to tear at the edges as a second, shadowy figure appeared on the shattered balcony. An icy hand gripped Matt's heart.

*One second more. Just one second more...*

The shadowy figure had seen him. Now it was standing directly in front of him, trying to get into his mind...

Matt backed up against the wall, but he had nowhere to go. His fingers were still moving, but slower now, his imagination losing its grip on the past. He sketched on, desperately, his blood dripping freely on to the paper. He fought the figure off with every part of his mind, using his blood as ink to capture its eyes. The figure reached towards him, trying to grab his sketchpad, the ghastly stumps of three fingers touching Matt's skin.

The past was reaching through to the present. Matt lurched from it. Then the palace crumbled and was lost once again. Gratefully, he let it happen.

Lying on his back, he looked up at the treetops, watching the flashes of sunlight slicing through their canopy. He exhaled slowly, letting the adrenalin filter from his system, trying not to see the boy and the butcher's knife, knowing he would see them forever.

He slowly sat up, closed his sketchpad and shoved it into his backpack.

*Em, I'm finished.*

*Em?*

## 54.

# IN CHAINS

Rémy hadn't gone down as fast as Em. He had managed to get his harmonica to his lips, but the flies had engulfed him in a cyclone of sticky blackness, knocking the instrument from his hands and flattening him to the ground, pressing his face into the red clay.

*Mom... Tia Rosa...*

Then the swarming darkness had carried Rémy Dupree Rush to a very bad place.

Rémy was naked, his clothes and the golden tablet gone, his eyelids crusted over with flies he'd crushed before he'd gone down. He tried to lift his hands to wipe his face, but found he couldn't move them thanks to the heavy iron chains cuffing his wrists. His knees were bent, and his ankles were cuffed like his wrists. He shifted his body, slipping against a cold, hard, tiled surface. He couldn't swallow, let alone sing. The ball gag and tape covering his lips saw to that.

Rolling to his left and then to his right, he tried to get a sense of how much mobility he had. A warm breeze from above brushed across his skin. It smelled of oranges. He could hear distant male voices arguing in Spanish. A small engine plane flew overhead. A dog barked. A car started up.

Rémy's eyes began to water as his anxiety rose. A sweat of fear coated his skin, making the tiled surface more slippery. The voices were coming closer. Two men were arguing. Rémy wished he'd paid more attention in Spanish class, but he had always been rehearsing a piece of music or a song in his head.

The crust over his eyes crumbled as he teased them open. He was in a stone cellar, a wall of aged barrels on his left and rows and rows of bottles, covered in cobwebs and a layer of thick dust, on his right. A set of wide plank stairs led straight up to a wooden door. His only source of air or light was a small, barred window.

Despite the chill and damp in the cellar, his skin was on fire and his limbs were cramping to the point of serious pain. When he tried to stretch his legs, his knees twisted and pain shot up into his lower back. He'd clearly been here for a while. He glanced over his shoulder and rocked in horror, tugging violently against his chains. A surgeon's tray with a flat razor sat behind his head.

From outside the barred window, the voices were coming closer. Rémy struggled against the manacles.

*You're stronger than me, baby boy. You always have been...*

He squeezed back the tears. Looking through the window, he saw legs, then a hand reaching down between the bars. He used his tongue to push the ball forward against the back of his teeth, willing himself not to gag. He couldn't make any sound from his throat.

Outside, one of the men said something that sounded important. Rémy thought he heard the word *sueño* – sleep.

Rémy moaned as a gas canister came flying through the space between the bars.

As darkness descended, he hoped they were talking literally.

## 55.

# GUILT TRIP

Matt climbed slowly to his feet, thousands of floaters in a rainbow of colours exploding in his peripheral vision. His stomach rolled. His scalp tingled. He leaned against the wall, letting a wave of nausea crash over him. His nose and eyes had stopped bleeding. That was something.

*Em, can you hear me?*

Nothing.

When he was steady enough on his feet, he grabbed his backpack and ran unsteadily through the collapsed gates of the palace and out into the scrub brush bordering the road, where he spotted an old yellow Ford pick-up truck abandoned in the ditch up ahead.

He threw open the driver's door, but it was empty.

Then suddenly he felt Em's presence. He darted to the back of the truck and stood up on the bumper. Em was tied up in the back.

*Matt? Oh, Matt. They took Rémy.*

Matt jumped into the truck's bed, untied his twin and helped her sit up. She had a nasty road rash on her legs where she'd been dragged, and she was covered in a disgusting bluish-black substance with the distinct metallic odour of blood.

'What happened here?'

'They took him,' said Em, throwing off the ropes once Matt had loosened them.

'That bastard Don Grigori was waiting for us. It was a trap to take Rémy. He knew we were here and he overwhelmed us both. I didn't have time to animate before they knocked me out, and Rémy didn't stand a chance.'

'How did they track us?' Matt asked.

'Someone must have told them we were coming here,' Em said shakily. 'I thought it might have been Caravaggio, but he's drinking at the Scottish seaside. Isn't he? He has no idea what we're doing.'

Matt rubbed his earlobe with one hand awkwardly. 'Um, yeah, about that…'

Em stared. 'Matt! What did you do?'

Matt had never felt more uncomfortable in his life.

'I wanted more information on the Camarilla, and he was the only one who seems to know anything about them.'

'When did you contact him?'

'I may have made a quick fade back to Scotland when you and Rémy were sleeping yesterday.'

'You talked to him?' said Em. 'You told him where we were going?'

'It might have slipped out, yes.' Matt flushed. To be honest, they hadn't done much talking.

Em slumped down on to the road. 'I've no words.'

Matt crouched in front of her, trying to ignore the wave of guilt rising in his gut.

'Caravaggio's a rogue and a narcissist, Em, and who knows what else, but he's not evil. We're dealing with evil here. If I can feel it, you can too.'

Em glanced around the barren landscape. 'That's why there's no wildlife.' She brushed off her scraped legs. 'We have to find Rémy. I think… I know they're going to do something terrible to him.'

Matt squeezed his sister's hand. Blaming themselves wasn't going to help find Rémy, and that was their first priority. He climbed into the driver's side of the truck.

'Get in,' he said.

Em jumped shotgun.

'They could have taken him anywhere,' she said as Matt got the truck started on his third attempt. 'If they have an Animare helping them, they could be long gone.'

'We're going inside that taverna in Olivera and you're going to inspirit the hell out of whoever is in there,' said Matt. 'Find out where he could be.'

He scraped the gears as he spun the truck 180 degrees. They sped to the village, tense and silent.

The place was empty.

'There's no one here,' said Em in despair before they

had even stepped out of the truck. 'There's no one any-where. It's a bloody ghost town. Now what?'

Matt let the engine idle while he pulled his sketchpad from his backpack.

'Do you recognize anyone from these drawings? They might help us figure out where they've taken Rémy.'

Em's eyes lit up. 'Mattie, it worked! I knew it would.'

She set the pad on her lap and flipped to the first of Matt's sketches: an image of the artist at the top of the steps in the rubble, his face looking out towards Matt.

'Well?' Matt asked hopefully.

Em shook her head. 'I don't recognize him, but Vaughn might.'

Matt turned to his third sketch, where he had cap-tured the artist leaving the building carrying a box under his arm. In the top corner of the page, he had sketched a close-up section of the artist.

'What do you think about this one?' he said. 'I have no memory of drawing it, but I must have.'

For the first time since she'd come to in the back of the truck, Em looked closely at her brother. His hair was unkempt on his shoulders. The whites of his eyes were bloodshot and his irises were full and black and laced with a web of gold, rather than his usual kaleidoscope of brilliant colours.

'Are you OK?'

'I'm fine.' Matt rubbed his eyes, then dropped his shades over them. 'I don't remember drawing so close up, that's all. Check out the symbol on the side of the box.'

Em looked at the drawing again. The box was made from unfinished wood and looked as if it had been constructed in a hurry. The sides were uneven in length and the nails holding it all together were misshapen, but the symbol on the seal was clear.

'It's the same as Rémy's birthmark,' she said in astonishment.

'Whatever is in that box has something to do with Rémy's powers as a Conjuror,' said Matt. 'And I'll bet you a million quid that Don Grigori wants... needs it.'

Em flipped back through the sketchpad, landing on a series of drawings that looked like early Kandinskys: swirls of dark limbs and bloody water. She flinched. The pain Matt had captured in his sketch was palpable. Em could feel it shooting into her fingers when she touched the drawing.

'God, Matt. What did you see?'

'Those red scarab tiles? They were from a big tiled bath, like a pool. There was a naked boy in the water, and a butcher with a knife—'

Em turned white. 'Stop,' she said. She turned to the sketches of the tall man with the knives strapped to his chest. 'Who was this?'

'I think this might be the Moor that Rémy's looking for. The one Rémy's mum said would help him.'

Exhausted, Em leaned back in the lumpy worn seat.

'If Animare are protecting Don Grigori and the Grand Inquisitor, then this Moor probably has someone protecting him too. We need to find him.'

'We need to contact Vaughn,' Matt said.

'With what?' said Em. 'We left our phones in the locker at Seville.'

'Not all of them.' Matt slipped one of the Orion flip-phones out of the front pocket of his jeans. He'd kept the flip-phone in his pocket because it had no GPS capabilities. 'Shit, no bars. Why am I not surprised?'

'Drive back up the hill towards Seville,' said Em, grabbing the phone and typing out a series of text messages. 'If we pass through an area with reception, texts will go through faster than phone calls.'

She snapped a few quick pictures of the faces from Matt's sketchpad, then glanced at her brother.

'You realize if you've been carrying this phone since Seville, someone in Orion may have tracked us and betrayed us to the Camarilla.'

Matt looked relieved. 'So it may not have been Caravaggio at all?'

'You're not off the hook yet,' said Em witheringly. 'But it's a possibility.'

'Fuck! Someone stole your car,' Matt observed as they pulled the truck away from the kerb, nodding at the space beside the tavern where the red convertible had been parked.

'Yup,' said Em, digging the sketch from her bag. 'And

if we're lucky, whoever it was is trying to pass a monster lorry on the motorway.' She tore up her drawing. 'Right about now.'

# 56.

# THE SECOND KINGDOM

The old Ford made it to the top of the hill and about another five kilometres before it sputtered to a stop. Swearing, Matt put the truck in neutral and manoeuvred it off the narrow road and under a copse of trees. It was dark now, and the last vehicle they'd seen – a Fiat packed with camping gear and an elderly couple who waved and smiled as they passed – had been a while ago.

Em yawned. 'Are we there yet?'

'Close,' said Matt. 'Maybe a few kilometres from the main road that'll take us to Seville, but I think we're going to need another vehicle. Gimme a sec. I'll take a look at the engine, see if I can figure out the problem. Otherwise, I'll animate something.'

'OK,' said Em sleepily. 'Be careful out there.'

Matt stared at his sister, at the way her eyelids were drooping.

'You really pick your moments to nap, Em,' he said. 'In case you've forgotten, we're trying to save Rémy's life.'

'Sorry,' Em mumbled. 'It's just... I feel so calm and comfortable.' She giggled faintly. 'Even with the smell of petrol seeping in from the dashboard and the springs stabbing me through the seat.'

Matt outlined a torch in his sketchpad, ignoring the pages of images from earlier in the day. He did his best to peer at the engine using the animation's faint light. Behind him, the high brush whistled in the warm night breeze, carrying with it the smell of manure and the sound of something big rushing across the field towards them.

Matt whirled round, and stared up into the dark face of a man seated on a huge black horse.

'My deepest apologies for your sister's forced siesta,' said the man, jumping from the saddle-less horse with an ease that belied his size.

'Since I could not be sure of your reaction to my sudden appearance, I decided encountering you one at a time might be the safest course of action. I am Don Alessandro de Mendoza,' said the man with a bow. 'But many know me as the Moor of Cadiz.'

Matt didn't reply right away. He just gawked. The Moor looked exactly as he had sketched him only hours earlier, climbing from the rubble of the Grand Inquisitor's palace with the body of a small boy on his back. But instead of torn robes and breeches, he looked like he was heading to a rodeo or to perform for a country rock band, in black jeans, a black cowboy shirt with silver buttons and shiny black cowboy boots. He still had his knives, though.

One in particular caught Matt's eye, its black handle etched with the symbol Rémy bore on his neck, its sharp blade tucked into a leather sheath at the man's hip. He didn't look any older than when Matt witnessed his escape from the rubble, which meant, if Matt's calculations were accurate, the man was at least five centuries old but didn't look a day over thirty.

'Matt Calder,' said Matt after a moment, extending his hand. The Moor shook it warmly. 'My sister is Em. We've been looking for you, sir.'

'And I you,' said the Moor. 'I lost you in London. I had to follow you here by more traditional means. Airplane travel is a difficult experience for me. Even after all these years in the twenty-first century, I find it terrifying.'

'You were in London?' Matt asked. 'Rémy was looking for you there.'

'He found me,' said the Moor. 'In a way.'

'But how did you find us?' Matt wanted to know.

The Moor studied Matt in the glimmer of the animated torch. With his pale skin and black clothing, the young man seemed half of the world and half not. The Moor gazed at Matt's dark irises laced with threads of gold, but as he was a man who had lived during an age of miracles and magic, he didn't comment.

'You and your sister have an unusual combination of powers,' he said.

'You have no idea,' said Matt.

'You leave certain auras in your wake. Over the years, I've become quite sensitive to auras.'

'You're a Guardian,' Matt said. 'Aren't you? Otherwise, Em wouldn't be snoring inside the truck right now.'

The Moor gently banged his hand against the door, startling Em awake. It took her a beat to take in the scene outside before she pushed open the cab door. The Moor helped her down then, before releasing her hand, he kissed it gently.

'I hope this way of greeting is still acceptable,' he said. 'It's a very long time since I've been in the company of such a powerful woman.'

'That way of greeting should always be acceptable,' Em said, staring up at the Moor's eyes. 'I recognize you from Matt's drawings. I am so happy to meet you. Have you been following us?'

'I have been watching over Rémy since he arrived in London, but you all left faster than I had anticipated,' said the Moor apologetically. 'Without an Animare by my side, I cannot travel quite as quickly. But that is a story for another time.'

From a distant bend on the mountain road, Matt spotted headlights coming towards them. The Moor led his horse behind the trees and tied him up before helping the twins push the truck out of sight. They climbed up into the flatbed and hid until the car had shot past. Then Em and Matt filled the Moor in on what had happened to Rémy, and what they had discovered from Matt's flashback.

'I should have come more quickly,' the Moor said fretfully. 'I've taken too many risks with that young man's existence.'

Heat lightning streaked across the sky above them.

'Are you Rémy's dad?' Em asked. Matt scowled at her.

*Jesus, Em.*

*I'm just asking. It's possible, don't you think?*

The Moor's expression was sombre. 'My children perished in another age,' he said. 'But it has been my sworn duty for centuries to protect those with the mark of the Conjuror, just as it has been the will of Don Grigori and the Grand Inquisitor to kill or enslave them and use their power for their own survival. I was protecting a Conjuror that day, the day you saw in your sketchpad, Matt.'

'The little boy?'

'I rescued him that day, but lost him to vile treachery,' said the Moor. 'He was a son to me, and yet someone I trusted betrayed us and he was enslaved and put on board a ship bound for Hispaniola, for the plantations. I never saw him again.'

'That's awful,' said Em, with tears in her eyes.

The Moor's voice grew quieter. 'It took me many years to recover from his loss. I rested among people who understood and protected me as I wondered how to make amends. I vowed then that while I had failed the boy, I would not fail his descendants. I searched for centuries until I found the Duprees. The mark was upon them. I fell to my knees and thanked my God for his mercy.'

'Who did you find?' asked Em. 'Rémy's mother?'

'Rémy's grandfather. My attentions, alas, were unwanted. He believed I was the Devil.' The Moor looked wry. 'I kept watch just the same. I learned to blend into the background. I guarded Rémy's mother from the day that she was born. As the fates would have it, I was with her the day that the Camarilla recognized her at a concert in London, when she was still in her youth.' He laughed bitterly. 'But she gave me the slip. Love, I believe, was the cause.'

'Rémy said his dad met his mum at a London concert,' said Em.

The Moor nodded.

'I persuaded her to leave London, return to the New World. I had hoped she and her new husband would be safe at her family home in Louisiana. But it seems that it was the worst place I could have sent her.'

'The painting,' said Em.

'The painting,' the Moor agreed. 'I had sent her to the heart of the viper's nest. For the one thing I did not know was that the Camarilla had sent the painting as cargo on the same slave ship as the Conjuror. Twice I have failed Rémy's family. I will not fail him again.'

Em stepped away from the lorry and looked up at the wisps of clouds skirting across the pale yellow moon. For a split second she couldn't help wondering if Zach was sitting on the jetty in Auchinmurn staring at the same moon. Had she made a mistake in following her brother instead of her heart? Em cut off the thread of these thoughts. Regrets were dangerous.

She turned back to the Moor, who was watching her intently.

'We've read parts of Annie Dupree's journal and we've heard Rémy's story,' she said. 'But what I still don't understand is who Don Grigori and the Grand Inquisitor are, or what they want.'

The wind rustled the trees noisily, the air warm and heavy. Thunder rumbled in the distance as more lightning shot through the sky, illuminating the red mountains.

'These beings are more dangerous than you can possibly imagine,' said the Moor. 'Centuries of hunting them has taught me that much.'

'Beings?' Matt said. 'As in, not human?'

'Don Grigori may once have been human,' the Moor said. 'But the Grand Inquisitor is from the beginning of everything, a divinity drawn from the darkness and formed in chaos. Some have said he is a fallen angel, banished from heaven when God created his kingdom on Earth. Others believe he is Orcus, ruler of the underworld.'

Matt squeezed Em's hand to squelch his rising terror. Em squeezed back, harder.

'When the Grand Inquisitor is loose in the world,' the Moor continued, 'his power exceeds that of all the Animare and Guardians put together. Time is a blink of an eye to him. And he has a wicked plan.'

'What is it?' said Matt, trying to prevent his voice from trembling.

'With the help of his Camarilla, the Grand Inquisitor is preparing Earth for something called the Second Kingdom. And the only one who can stop him is a Conjuror.'

Three long fingers of lightning shot across the sky, illuminating the curve of the narrow road and the scrub brush. In that split second, Matt saw four men in commando gear with masks and night-vision goggles, crawling in the scrub towards the truck. They were carrying guns and gas canisters.

'Camarilla!' Matt shouted.

The Moor's head snapped round. Before Matt and Em could react, he had torn the night goggles from one man's face and broken another's forearm with a snap kick. A gun fell at the howling man's feet. The Moor kicked it into the brush.

But as fast as the Moor's movements were, he wasn't

fast enough. Even as he whirled about to fight off the third attacker, a canister of gas flew through the air, rolled on to the bed of the truck and released its poison.

# 57.

# CAPTIVES

As soon as Matt had regained consciousness, he wished he hadn't. He stared at the liquid sloshing around his naked chest. He was chained and appeared to be sitting in a pool of warm water. He looked down and shifted from barbed calm to full-on panic when he saw blood in the water. Reaching into the water, he checked he was still in one piece, finding two distinct things that returned his emotional state to one of mild terror.

He was not alone in the tiled pool.

The blood was not his.

Chained at the opposite side of the tiled bath with a bad cut on his forearm, was Rémy, his blood twisting in the water like hundreds of scarlet snakes. A ball gag was shoved deep into his mouth.

Matt started moving, shifting his body forward and back, trying to generate waves with enough power to splash Rémy's face and wake him. Rémy groaned and moved.

So he wasn't dead – yet.

Two of them might have a better chance of escaping than one alone.

But where was Em? If she was free, then their chances of escape from this horror were even better.

Rémy moaned. He lifted his head, before it lolled on to his chest again.

*It's dark outside. It has to be between ten and eleven.*

Rémy moaned again. This time, he raised his head and stared across the pool as if in a trance. Matt watched his eyes squint and then open wide as he realized that he was not alone.

Matt called out tentatively in his mind.

*Em, can you hear me?*

For the second time that day, he got no answer.

Rémy's eyes were red-rimmed and one side of his cheek was puffy and covered in dried blood. He must have put up a fight when the vicious gag had been put in place. They stared at each other across the water.

Matt concentrated on Rémy's emotions, reading his rapid heart rate, his intense surge of feelings, and did his best to interpret them. Focusing on someone else's situation kept him from reflecting on the fact that he shared the same predicament.

'We all walked into a trap,' Matt said as gently as he could. 'They knew we were coming.'

Rémy shook his head. He tried to shift the ball to the front of his mouth again, but only succeeded in getting it lodged further back in his throat, sending him into a paroxysm of coughing. He slipped further down into the water.

'We met the Moor on the road to Seville,' Matt went on. 'Well, he kind of met us. But then Don Grigori and the Camarilla found us. He and Em are here somewhere, I think. I hope.'

*Em?*

Still no response.

Matt spotted the tray and the surgical utensils on the table behind Rémy. In a surge of horror, he wrenched madly at the manacles on his ankles and wrists.

*Mattie?! Are you OK? Your panic is making me sick.*

Matt had never been so glad to hear his sister's voice in his life.

*Em, thank God. We have to get out of here before Don Grigori shows up to slice up our privates. Where are you?*

*Not sure. I'm in chains. In a cellar, I think. It's hard for me to see. It's so dark. Don Grigori obviously doesn't know we're telepathic or he would have kept one of us unconscious. So there's that.*

*Oh good. You'll be able to hear my silent screams.*

\*

Across the other side of the pool, Rémy struggled to get Matt's attention. He guessed Matt was talking to his sister in his head. He took some comfort from that.

'Em's fine,' said Matt, noticing Rémy's expression. 'Can you use your voice at all?'

Rémy shook his head. He tried to hum and the pain that shot through his jaw was like a knife in his brain. He wondered if they had broken his jaw when they strapped him up. It felt as if his mouth was on fire.

'No worries, man. We'll think of another way.'

Rémy watched as Matt ran his fingers along the rough tiles that lined the pool. It looked like he was trying to dislodge a piece of tile, perhaps to scratch out some kind of image. But whoever owned this place had kept these baths in perfect condition, and he wasn't having much luck.

The quiet of the bath was interrupted by the electric buzz of a thousand flies, growing louder, as if a missile was about to crash through the cellar walls. Matt yanked on his chains frantically. Rémy did the same.

Big wet bluebottles swarmed into the cellar through every crevice and crack in the stone walls. They surged through the barred windows and the openings around the door. They hovered around the ceiling, swirled round the oak barrels and, in seconds, carpeted the floor and papered the walls in hissing, sucking blackness.

The cellar door opened and Don Grigori floated down the plank steps. Rage shot adrenalin into Rémy's every muscle. He rattled his chains with fury and tried to yell, pushing sounds up from his chest, but nothing. Only more pain in his jaw and his already aching limbs. He no longer saw the man on the outside, but the murderous monster Don Grigori had become. Instead of perfect coiffed blond hair, Rémy saw Medusa's locks of coiling black snakes. Don Grigori's head and face were a series of sharp flat planes and soft decaying angles, not so much a face any more as a dark hollow.

But it was the sound of the pipe that broke him, cutting into his mind and tearing open his soul. The pipe held the keening of all the families Don Grigori had destroyed, all the voices he had silenced and the lives he had cut short. The *castrato* was a satellite, broadcasting the anguish of past, present and future: mothers pleading for their children, men begging for sons, children crying out for anyone to save them from the horror. Then the keening became his mother's voice, singing her very last song as she dangled from the edge of the broken balcony, covered in flies.

*You are my sunshine…*

Rémy made one more furious attempt to wrench free, his howls choking in his throat. Tears streamed down his face.

*I'm sorry, Mom… I wasn't stronger than you after all.*

*That's enough, both of you. He hasn't cut off your balls yet!*

Rémy's head snapped up. Perhaps his mind had

cracked like his mother's, but he could swear he'd just heard Em in his head.

Matt stared at him across the water.

*Rémy, did you just hear Em? Can you hear me?*

Rémy looked across the pool at Matt and nodded.

Em's voice came again. *Say something, Rémy.*

Rémy fought the shrilling sound of Don Grigori's pipe, the buzzing of the flies.

*Can you... hear me? Em? Matt?*

Matt sagged a little against the bath.

*We hear you.*

Rémy looked at him in wonder. *I've only heard music in my imagination my whole life. I can hear your words as if they were notes of music.*

*Good enough for me,* Em's voice replied. *I'm working on a plan. Stay tuned.*

Rémy prayed Em was right as Don Grigori floated behind him and lifted the straight razor from the tray. He dipped it into the warm water and stood with it over Rémy's head.

'Your escape from me in Chicago was a costly mistake,' the *castrato* murmured in his honeyed, high-pitched voice. 'I failed to factor in your aunt. More fool me. But she is gone now, as is your mother. There is no one left to help you.'

Rémy blazed hatred at the creature before him. Don Grigori laughed.

'Of course, your mother should have destroyed

the painting when she had the chance, that day in the archives. But she wasted the day sobbing for her poor husband, lost so tragically beneath the wheels of that skidding car. If she'd been a little stronger, she might have stopped us back then.'

He switched his gaze to Matt.

'It was clumsy of you and your sister to animate in our vault in Old Worm's that day. Did you think us so foolish as not to be prepared for such a breech? We have been watching you ever since. But before I despatch you, I have promised your suffering to a friend.'

A man with bushy eyebrows and a baggy old cardigan jogged down the wooden steps and over to Don Grigori, carrying a set of clean white robes and a leather strop. He set the robes reverentially on a bench near the oak barrels. Rémy recognized him as one of the clerks from the shop.

'Thank you, Hector.' Don Grigori slipped into the robes and took the leather strop from the man's out-stretched hands. He sharpened the razor against it. 'I will try to be accurate and swift in my cuts.'

'You can kill us,' said Matt shakily, 'but you won't last long once we're gone. Every Animare and Guardian will be after you and your Camarilla. They'll destroy you all.'

'I've escaped this world more times than you'll ever know,' Don Grigori murmured. 'I feel quite confident that I will do it again.'

In a flash, the *castrato* was in the water and on top of Rémy, his legs astride Rémy's naked body, his robes floating out behind him in the water. Rémy flailed against the chains, the invasion, rusty manacles cutting his skin, his blood swirling into the fly-infested water.

Don Grigori twisted Rémy's head to look at the Conjuror's mark. Then he stretched down into the water and gently, obscenely, cupped Rémy's genitals in his cold, thin fingers. Rémy railed against the assault.

Grinning, Don Grigori squeezed.

'A fighter. Like the last one of your kind that I despatched so poetically aboard his lost and forsaken ship. Your mother was a fighter too.'

The mention of his mother was all the spark Rémy needed to ignite Em's plan. The *castrato* lifted the razor above his head. Rémy closed his eyes and opened his mind to Em and Matt. Their imaginations fused into one blinding source of power.

The water began to bubble and steam rose from its depth. The flies rose off the pool all at once and swarmed above the scene in confusion and uncertainty. And Don Grigori paused, startled, as Matt began to sing in a husky croon.

'What—'

Rémy's chains snapped on his arms first. He stabbed his fingers deep into the *castrato*'s eyes, grabbed his hair and plunged his head under the water. While Don Grigori gasped and groped to the surface, Rémy dislodged the

JOHN & CAROLE BARROWMAN

ball gag. With a triumphant howl, he shattered Matt's
manacles. Matt was out of the bath in a flash and laying
a punch square on Hector's jaw, the flies swarming up
from every surface and attacking his naked body, leach-
ing on to his skin in a sticky mass.

*Keep singing!*

Don Grigori reared out of the water, gasping and
wrenching away from Rémy's grip. Rémy's song kept
the flies at bay, just like his mother's had in her final
moments. They swarmed instead round the *castrato*,
encasing and protecting him as he raised his pipe furiously to his lips and began to play. The water began to
boil and darken before Matt and Rémy's eyes. The flies
seemed to draw courage from the sound, dive-bomb-
ing Rémy again, filling his mouth and choking off the
music.

Nursing his jaw, Hector turned and scrambled for
the stairs. Matt was fast on Hector's heels, yanking him
back and knocking him out cold on the floor.

'Not so fast, you little shit...'

Rémy spat out the flies and sang louder. Long, web-
like cracks raced across the ceiling, raining dust and
rock on top of them. Don Grigori played harder. The
flies pressed down, filling every inch of space in the
cramped little room, squashing their fat, hungry bodies
against every part of Rémy and Matt.

*We need an exit, Em, and fast. Or we're going to
drown in flies!*

Don Grigori's pipe was inciting the torrent of flies as they dive-bombed every inch of space around Rémy, their bodies creating a wall that separated him from Matt.

*I'm working on it!*

# 58.

# THE FINAL CUT

Rémy's singing was rising in pitch. He was holding his notes longer, breathing more deeply, effortlessly filling the room with a heavy silver fog. Don Grigori tried to match the pitch of his pipe to Rémy's voice, his eyes burning with fear and loathing. The higher the wall of flies grew between him and Matt, the higher Rémy's voice soared. The flies fell from Matt's body like he was shedding his skin. With a growl of rage, Don Grigori played on, darkening and thickening the water in the pool to the smell and consistency of sulphurous tar.

*This is what hell smells like.*

'Keep going!' Matt shouted, swatting at the remaining flies. 'Rémy, you're winning!'

Don Grigori's pipe changed pitch. The tar rose up out of the pool in the shape of a great golem, eyes blazing red as if Don Grigori had made his evil visible. The flies encased the beast, their bodies merging, giving the creature great black wings so that it was able to lift itself from the pool and cover the ceiling. The beast's dark mass loomed above the boys, separating them from Don Grigori on the other side of the room.

Rémy felt Matt sketching in his wide-open mind, twisting the music into ink, marking out something cold and hard which materialized in his hand. A sword with a black handle, its blade etched with the Conjuror's mark. Next, a full set of black leather armour clothed Rémy from head to foot. Rémy lunged at the monster, swinging the blade, sending a limb-like chunk of tar flying against the wall, branding its shape into the cold, hard stone.

Matt stuck his fingers in the repulsive tar-like substance and began to draw for himself now, a set of medieval armour with a black-handled sword, its silver blade etched with the same mark.

*Looking sick, man...*

*Not letting you have all the fun...*

Rémy let his voice rise up to the heavens again. He slashed and lunged into the heart of the creature with his sword. The beast's eyes burned like the flames of an imagined hell. Rémy swung at them, detonating one glowing eyeball and sending it spattering in Matt's direction. It hit the ground with the sound of sizzling flesh.

Together they hacked their way into the belly of the beast. In seconds, they could see through to the cowering Don Grigori on the other side. They could see the panic strip the *castrato*'s face of all colour, his eyes darting from side to side, searching for a way out of this hell of his own making.

A thunderous rumbling shook the entire space as if they were at the epicentre of an earthquake. Chunks of plaster rained on them from above. The entire cellar groaned.

Rémy thought of his mother and her years of suffering and study. All for him. He thought of Tia Rosa and her life of sacrifice. All for him. And finally he thought of his dad, whom he had known so briefly, who had loved him and his mother more than his own life. His voice shifted to a growling version of Tia Rosa's favourite song.

> *'When you walk through a storm, hold your head*
>     *up high*
> *And don't be afraid of the dark…'*

A gigantic sucking hole opened in the floor beneath Don Grigori 's flyblown feet.

> *'Walk on, through the wind, walk on, through the*
>     *rain…'*

The *castrato* screamed, high and pathetic, as Rémy's sword paused over his heart.

'This is for all of us,' Rémy said, before hitting the song's climax.

> *'And you'll ne-e-e-ver wa-a-alk alo-o-one.'*

He hit high C.

Don Grigori's head exploded at the exact moment Em crashed through the wall in a shiny pink army tank, and almost killed them all.

# 59.

# REUNION

Three hours later, Matt and Rémy, still clothed in their black leather armour, sat on the benches of a decorative wooden gazebo with sides that had been laser-cut to resemble trees made of musical notes. The gazebo was situated in the centre of a lush garden, the laurel hedging of which was trimmed to afford an entertaining view of the chaos unfolding on the paved, circular driveway to El Parador de Montaña Roja, a luxury hotel on the edge of Olivera. The hotel had been constructed around an original sixteenth-century palace. Or, at least, what was left of it.

Three fire engines, a battalion of uniformed police, four gents in black suits and open-necked white shirts and a host of irate hotel guests were all staring at the smouldering remains of the hotel's oldest and most expensive wing.

'It was beautiful here once,' said the Moor, joining the boys. 'When the Grand Inquisitor took my castle from me, I built this instead. The gardens were full of birdsong and beautiful creatures. Now all is smoke and ruin. Such are the trials of time.' He stared a little sadly at the wreckage. 'I had forgotten that those barrels in the cellars contained gunpowder. You would think it had lost its bang in the intervening years.'

'Apparently not,' said Matt.

Rémy startled from his half-doze. 'Professor?' he said in astonishment. 'Your voice... your beard? You've bathed? I don't understand... How—'

The Moor cut gently through Rémy's stammered questions. 'Forgive the deception. My many guises were to protect you.'

'You're the Moor! Why didn't you tell me sooner?'

'I let you fulfil your mother's final wishes, God rest her soul.'

Rémy threw himself into the Moor's open arms. The Moor held him against his chest for a few seconds before kissing each cheek.

'I found you after all,' Rémy said in wonder.

'Indeed. Although you seemed to manage without me very well.' The Moor smiled. 'Your mother would be proud of all that you have accomplished.'

He placed his hands on Rémy's shoulders.

'I am sorry for not making myself known to you sooner. First of all, I needed to be sure it was you, and, second, I'd promised Annie to keep a watch over you, but not to draw you into a battle that was not yet yours, especially one I wasn't sure we... you could win.'

'We can win this,' said Rémy with conviction.

'He has more help now,' said Matt. 'The Grand Inquisitor has his Camarilla. The Conjuror has the Calder twins.'

For a beat, Rémy and Matt wavered between a fist-bump and a high-five. They embraced instead.

The Moor withdrew from his pocket the golden tablet that Don Grigori had taken from Rémy. He slipped the leather string over Rémy's head so that the warm metal rested against Rémy's chest once again.

'I gave half of this to a young boy, the first Conjuror I failed to protect, all those centuries ago, as a talisman and a promise of my fealty,' he said. 'It's been in your family line ever since. And with it, my pledge still stands.'

'Thank you,' said Rémy. He touched his tablet, his talisman. 'It knew where the portrait was.'

'The portrait is no longer in Old Worm's,' said the Moor, his eyes hooded and his tone full of concern. 'We must find it again quickly before the Grand Inquisitor can be released again.'

'Lucky your painting was in London for that exhibition,' said Matt.

'Luck,' said the Moor with a smile, patting Matt on the shoulder, 'had little to do with it. Just as the Grand Inquisitor has his Camarilla, I too have valuable friends.'

'Are you going to take this place back?' Matt gestured at the gardens, and the palatial hotel. 'It's yours, after all.'

'One day,' said the Moor. 'But it will require careful planning. This world has thought me dead for a very long time, after all.'

Footsteps approached on the secluded path behind the gazebo, coming from the direction of the stables. Rémy and Matt leaped to their feet, nerves frayed and perceptions still heightened.

Em stepped inside the gazebo and grinned at them.

'So, a shiny pink army tank, Em,' Matt said, relaxing again. 'Really?'

Em threw herself between Matt and Rémy on the bench. 'All I had in my pocket was a melted lipgloss. What can I say?'

# 60.

# INTRODUCTIONS

Em's flip-phone pinged.

'Finally, service,' she said, glancing at the screen. 'It's from Vaughn. He says he's on his way.'

Matt stared at the people by the front of the hotel. 'He's here already. Look.'

Vaughn stood among the police and hotel guests. A tall dark-haired young woman stood with him.

'Who's with him?' Rémy asked.

'Hope it's not Mum,' said Em.

Vaughn broke into a jog towards them, his face set in a frown the twins knew a little too well. The woman kept pace with him, although she took a more sedate route than Vaughn, who simply hurdled the low hedges of the garden. The gazebo was becoming less and less like a quiet spot for romantic interludes and more and more like a crowded bus shelter.

'My God,' Vaughn growled, pulling Em and Matt into angry hugs, 'you two will be the death of me. What were you thinking? I sent you on a simple job. You nearly get yourselves killed!'

He shook Rémy's hand with a swift nod, and looked curiously at the Moor.

'Lakshmi,' he said to his female companion, 'meet my reprobate trainees, Matt and Em Calder. And Rémy Dupree Rush too, of course. This is Lakshmi Misra, from the Metropolitan Police.'

'You're the police officer at Old Worm's,' Rémy said, staring at Lakshmi.

'I remember you too,' said Matt. 'Em and I followed you to South Kensington.'

Lakshmi lifted her shoulders apologetically. 'There was no other way to get you across the city to where you needed to be. Rémy was there with Alessandro's portrait, and I knew he needed your help.'

'Señor Grant,' said the Moor, bowing slightly. 'Don Alessandro de Mendoza, the Moor of Cadiz. I've heard a great deal about you and your organization over the years. Truth be told, if not for your fine young agents, we would all be in a lamentable state. And my dear Lakshmi! Is my portrait safe? I had no choice but to abandon it.'

'The curators were a little stunned,' said Lakshmi, 'but Papa has covered your tracks, and I was able to contact Vaughn and explain what was happening. He was already concerned for the twins' safety, so I invited him to travel with me.'

'Is this the first time you've worked together?' asked Rémy.

Lakshmi smiled. 'I've had Orion's number for a long time, but I've never had to use it until this week.'

'So you lied to us earlier when you said Orion knew about the Camarilla and the painting,' said Em, her hands on her hips.

'I'm sorry, Em, but at that moment things were on a need-to-know basis. You both are still on probation after all.'

'I'm impressed,' said Matt, grinning and slapping Vaughn on the shoulder.

'With what?' said Vaughn, eying him suspiciously.

'With the fact that you were able to keep a lie from Em's Guardian senses.'

'Thank you,' smiled Vaughn. 'I've been practising.'

'I need a lesson or two,' said Matt.

# 61

# STREET FIGHTING MAN

The following morning, Matt, Em, Rémy and the Moor sat on the balcony of a small bed and breakfast on a leafy cobbled street off Seville's main square. Vaughn had already returned to London with Lakshmi, to meet with the European Council of Guardians and enlighten them on Rémy's existence. The same artist who ran the gallery through which Em, Matt and Rémy had faded two days ago owned the bed and breakfast, which for the time being was closed to other guests.

The dishes from breakfast had been cleared and only coffee cups and an assortment of water and juice glasses remained. The balcony was in the shade as it was still early and the streets around the square were quiet. Shopkeepers were sweeping their stoops and hosing the previous night's debris into the sewers, preparing for the first wave of tourists.

The smells of coffee and warm bread reminded Rémy of Tia Rosa. He swallowed hard.

'Grief comes in waves,' Em said, watching him. 'The waves take your breath away some days. Other days, you can ride them.'

Rémy smiled and swirled the coffee in his cup. 'Are your waves getting smaller?'

'A little. Maybe,' Em replied. 'But my grief's a bit different. Zach's not dead. Just gone.'

Once the table was cleared, Matt spread out his sketches from the Grand Inquisitor's ruined palace. The Moor examined them closely.

'An amazing likeness. This man,' he said, pointing at the artist Matt had captured climbing from the debris. 'He may have been the true hero of the day.'

'Who is he?' asked Matt.

'His name is Hieronymus Bosch, a brilliant artist and Animare. He and I had planned for the boy to incapacitate the Grand Inquisitor and Don Grigori with his voice, so that we could take the one thing the Grand Inquisitor has protected since he came into being. I failed in my part. He succeeded in his. For that, we can at least be grateful.'

Em tapped the object tucked up against the artist's tunic. 'Did his part have something to do with what's in this box?'

'That box contains the most sacred of all musical instruments,' said the Moor. 'The Lyre of Orpheus. When the lyre is played, it has the power to open the underworld.'

'*Musica vivificat mortuos*,' Rémy said softly. 'Music gives life to the dead.'

'Where is the lyre now?' Em asked. 'Where did Bosch hide it?'

'That,' said the Moor, 'is a very good question.'

'And, perhaps, that,' said Matt, sitting up, 'is why someone is stealing musical instruments from paintings. They're looking for the lyre.'

The sound of taxi and car horns and the rising voices of three arguing men rose to their table. The Moor leaned over the railing.

'Now, this reminds me of my time,' he said approvingly. 'Men fighting in the streets over their debts, or the love of a beautiful woman.'

Two of the men had knocked a third to the ground, who was now jumping to his feet and preparing to take both of them on. Men were bursting from nearby cafés to join the fray, three young women obviously related to one or more of the men jumping in the mix behind them. The commotion had blocked the narrow thoroughfare.

Abruptly, Matt vaulted over the balcony and landed on his feet in the middle of the chaos. Em, Rémy and the Moor watched in surprise as Matt punched, jabbed and dodged his way through the melee, heading into the thick of the brawl – where Em spotted a familiar figure, black curls blowing, wicked black eyes gleaming, fists flying.

'Perhaps we should give Matt some assistance,' said the Moor.

Someone from a balcony opposite shoved open their shutters, cranked their stereo and blasted out the Stones' 'Street Fightin' Man' from a set of cheap speakers to add to the atmosphere. From the other side of the square, police sirens cut through the sounds of battle, heading their way.

'I think I'll let Matt have all the fun,' said Rémy with a wince.

'Are you sure you're OK?' asked Em, her fingers touching his swollen jaw.

'More than I've been in a while.' He squeezed her hand.

Matt had reached Caravaggio now. He strong-armed the artist across the street, back to the door of the bed and breakfast, shoving him hard up the stairs and out on the balcony, throwing him to the ground at Em, Rémy and the Moor's feet.

'Why so serious, my little friend?' Caravaggio gave a drunken hiccup. One of his eyes was already swelling from a well-laid punch. 'S'only a fight…'

Without Caravaggio's input, the fighting was already morphing to energetic dancing. Taxis and cars were pulling up, disgorging crowds intent on joining the party.

'Keep him there, Em,' Matt ordered.

Em put her foot on Caravaggio's black-shirted chest, holding him down, until Matt returned to the balcony with a packet of frozen peas. He tossed them to Caravaggio, who pressed them to his eye.

'Vegetables are good for one thing only,' Caravaggio grinned. 'Painting.'

The Moor gazed curiously at Caravaggio. 'Michele?' he said. 'Is that you?'

'Alessandro!'

The Moor helped the artist to his feet. The men embraced with enthusiasm.

'Why am I not surprised they know each other?' said Em to Matt.

'Who is he?' asked Rémy.

Matt grabbed the frozen peas from Caravaggio and held them to his own bottom lip, which was already starting to puff up where he'd taken a glancing blow.

'This thug is Caravaggio, the bane of my Orion existence.'

'Caravaggio?' said Rémy. 'Like, the artist?'

'I am not *like* the artist,' said Caravaggio, leaning on the Moor for support and looking offended. 'I *am* the artist.'

'Are you hungry, Michele?' the Moor asked.

'He is not,' said Matt emphatically. 'His appetite is what got him the black eye.'

'A gold coin is worth nothing in this age,' Caravaggio complained. 'I simply offered a service to cover my meal and its taxes. The landlord was unwilling to barter.'

'How did you get away from Guthrie? You didn't hurt him, did you?' asked Em.

'Of course not!' said Caravaggio. 'I'd never hurt

another artist. I simply offered him a service in exchange for my freedom. Would you like details?'

'No!' said the twins in unison.

'Why are you here?' Matt asked.

Caravaggio wagged a finger. 'One good turn deserves another. You are hard to find, pretty boy. I have been drinking my way around half the cities in Spain in pursuit of you.'

'It's a hard life,' Em observed.

'I have news of a painting that gossip suggests you are trying to find,' Caravaggio declared. 'A double portrait, yes?'

'You've seen the portrait?' Rémy said, rising from his chair.

*Where the hell does he get his information from, Mattie?*

*Don't ask, Em. Just be grateful.*

'Tell us where it is, Caravaggio,' said Matt out loud.

'Somewhere ve-ery difficult to access,' the artist said. 'Somewhere, truth to tell, where I should not have been in the first place. But when has that ever stopped me?'

The Moor laughed. 'Never in my experience, Michele.'

'Where is the portrait?' said Rémy. 'Please, sir, this is very important.'

Caravaggio prodded Rémy on the chest. 'I like this boy. He has manners. The painting that you seek is in...' He paused, eyeing Matt and Em. 'Well now, I seem to have forgotten. Perhaps the offer of my continued freedom in the world might dislodge the memory?'

'You can have two months if you tell us,' said Em.

'Thank you, dear girl.' Caravaggio winked at Matt. 'You've always been my favourite.'

'The painting,' growled Matt.

'The portrait you seek is inside a vault beneath the Vatican City itself.'

# QUESTIONS FOR YOUR BOOK CLUB

- What did you think of Em, Matt and Rémy's special powers in the story? If you could draw one thing and have it come to life, what would it be?

- Rémy's musical abilities allow him to alter reality. If you could conjure using a specific skill, what would that skill be?

- Music and art are everywhere in this novel. Do you have a favourite painting or cherished song that you think would have a place in this story? What is it? Where would you put it in the story?

- Rémy's unusual gift often makes him feel like he isn't 'normal' and that he doesn't fit in with other teenagers. Do you know anyone who feels this way? How have you helped them?

- Have you ever experienced feeling different or alienated from those around you like Rémy? How did you overcome this?

- When Em is in Edinburgh shopping with her mum, they get into an awkward conversation about whether or not Em is pregnant. Have you ever been in a similar awkward conversation? How did you handle it?

- Do you think Matt made the right decision about not getting bound to an official Guardian?

- Do you think Em made the right decision at the Union Ceremony?

- In the story, Vaughn, Caravaggio and the twins are able to travel via famous paintings. Do you have a painting you'd like to 'fade' into?

- The novel contains a number of scary scenes, including the ending in the Spanish baths. What scenes in the novel did you find particularly dark?

- The first conjuror arrives in America on a slave ship. What do you know about slavery during the 17th and 18th centuries? Was slavery in the UK different from slavery in America?

- When Rémy gets to London, he's suddenly homeless. What are some of the lessons he learns as a homeless teenager? Do you know anyone who is homeless? What are some of the things your community is doing to assist homeless teens? What might you do?

- The phrase 'African diaspora' is used in the story to describe the relocation of Africans around the world as a result of the transatlantic slave trade. Can you think of other groups of people across history that this term describes?

- Where do you think Em, Matt and Rémy's story will lead them next?

# Q&A WITH THE AUTHORS

**1. What inspired the idea for *Conjuror*?**

JB: The initial idea came up a couple of years ago when Carole and I took a road trip with our husbands across Spain in a conversion van named Barry Vanilow. We seem to come up with our best ideas when we're on road trips. I think Animare to Conjuror was a logical creative leap... if that's a thing.

CB: It is now! To go from a superpower involving the twins' imaginations and art to Rémy's imagination conjuring reality with music just made sense. Plus John's lived in the world of music most of his life... From the beginning of our collaboration on this new series, we wanted at least one mixed-race character in a lead role. We spent a lot of time brainstorming Rèmy's backstory. The more we thought about him, his music and his family's history the more we realized Conjurors needed to come from a different mythology than the Celtic myths shaping our Hollow Earth series.

## 2. Which character in *Conjuror* do you feel the most similar to and why?

CB: I'm pretty sure there's a little of each character in both of us, especially their passion for art and music, how they challenge authority and how they're constantly questioning their so-called destiny.

JB: Agree.

CB: Seriously? No debate?

JB: Well, maybe I'd add that Em's choice to follow Matt to Orion and not stay with Zach – her choice to embrace an unknown future – is a risk I'd take... one I've taken a few times.

## 3. The twins are able to alter reality through art. If you could bring any work of art to life, what would it be?

JB: If I have to pick just one, I'd say Paul Delaroche's 'The Execution of Lady Jane Grey.' The lady-in-waiting in the background gets to me every time. She has her back to us with her hands up against the wall. The emotion she projects in her stance is heartbreaking and we can't even see her face! I just want to get in there and tell her she'll be OK.

CB: I love the Pre-Raphaelites. I'd want to sit in the canoe with the Lady of Shalott in John William Waterhouse's painting. According to Arthurian legend, she was locked away in a tower and was only able to weave the world she saw reflected in a mirror. I really want to see what's on that tapestry.

**4. The twins have shown us that working alongside a sibling can sometimes be tough! How do you find working together?**
CB: He's a nightmare.

JB: She's a challenge... actually both of these things can be true on occasion but, honestly, it's one of the joys of our collaborating that we're closer now than we've ever been.

CB: Aw... it also helps that we're often miles apart!

**5. Matt and Em are able to communicate through telepathic powers. Have you ever experienced any strange telepathic moments with each other?**
JB: Not sure it's telepathy, but it can be weird. Often a look or a gesture from either of us can trigger something. Sometimes if we are in a situation where we can be silly or a bit outrageous, I'll look at her and she'll know something's going to happen.

CB: At that point I usually just get out of the way... or join in.

**6. Do you have a specific writing process you stick to when working together? Who comes up with the wackiest ideas?**

JB: Our collaboration is heavier early in the process when we're brainstorming and outlining. Then Carole writes. She does most of the heavy lifting. I usually jump back in with notes after she has a solid draft. It's a collaboration that plays well to our strengths.

CB: If one of us has a crazy idea, it usually leads to something equally crazy from the other, which then leads to snorting-out-our-noses laughing and that often leads to something brilliant we can use in the book. We've learned laughter can be a great creative stimulant.

**7. There are many historical references within the story. What research did you have to do before writing *Conjuror*?**

CB: I did quite a bit after John and I outlined the plot, especially about the Moor in history and the beginnings of the Atlantic slave trade, but I'm more a researcher-on-demand. I jump into the writing immediately from our notes and when something comes up that demands research I do it.

JB: We're always making lists of paintings that would be cool to use in the series too, and right now we're researching music for the next books.

**8. What kind of books do you both enjoy reading? Are there any in particular that inspired the story for _Conjuror_?**

CB: For sure Anne Rice's _Cry To Heaven_ was an inspiration for _Conjuror_. Rice is amazing at creating chilling, seductive characters and writing elegant horror stories. I know our castrato was Rice inspired. We're huge fans of her writing.

JB: I'm reading scripts all the time which means I don't get through books as quickly as I'd like, but I love to read and I've always got a stack on my bedside table. I'm a huge geek and sci-fi fan. I have lots of comics, too, on my table and loaded on my iPad.

CB: I'm a voracious reader. It's a perk of my job as an English professor. I do my best to keep up across all genres. Like John, I'm a big sci-fi fan, and because I review crime fiction for a couple of US newspapers, I have to read four or five books in that genre most weeks.

**9. We've loved following Matt and Em's adventures since the Hollow Earth trilogy. What does the future hold for the twins? For Rémy? For the Moor?**

JB: The Camarilla will become even more of a threat, especially to Lakshmi who will have a bigger role in the next book.

CB: We'll see the three teenagers take greater risks with their powers as they pursue the portrait and investigate the prophecies about the Second Kingdom.

JB: I want to see Matt struggle with Caravaggio even more. I'm really looking forward to that!

CB: Ha! Me too.

JB: And since the Moor and Caravaggio already know each other, maybe they'll 'spar' a little too.

CB: If readers pay close attention to the foreshadowing in the opening chapters, they'll get a few strong clues about what's coming.

Thanks for taking this reading journey with us!
Carole & John
2016